DEATH IN WESTMINSTER

An Augusta Peel Mystery Book 5

EMILY ORGAN

The Augusta Peel Series

Chapter 1

'WHAT HAVE you got by Jane Austen?' asked an Irish lady dressed in blue. She had piercing eyes and a loud voice. A fox fur hung around her neck and her nose was red from the late February cold.

'The shelf for authors beginning with "A" is just there.' Augusta pointed to it.

'But what have you got?' The lady clearly didn't wish to look for herself.

'All of them I think. Which one are you looking for?'

'One I've not read.'

Augusta could feel her patience being tested. She stepped out from behind the counter of her bookshop and forced a smile. Then she stepped over to the shelf labelled "A".

'Here are all the books we have by Jane Austen.' She pointed at them. 'If you have a look at them, you might see one you haven't read.'

The Irishwoman squinted at the shelf and Augusta suspected she needed spectacles. Meanwhile, her attention turned to a man in a black overcoat. He was standing near the window, leafing through a book on British wildlife. His dark hair was combed back and long on his collar. He had a thin moustache and looked about twenty-five. Augusta had observed him leaf through several books over the past ten minutes. He had also climbed the staircase to the mezzanine floor twice and made some furtive glances at her. Perhaps he had some time to waste or was indecisive. Either way, he was making her uneasy.

'I've read all these,' announced the Irishwoman. 'Have you not got any more?'

'No. It seems you've read all of Jane Austen's books,' said Augusta.

'I don't think so. I can only see six here.'

'Jane Austen only wrote six books.'

'Is that all?'

'I'm sure she would have written more had she lived longer. She died at forty-one.'

'Forty-one? Poor woman.'

'Two of her novels were published after her death and I believe she was working on another which was never finished.'

'That's a shame. So what do I read now?'

'Have you read anything by the Brontë sisters?'

'No. Where are they?'

'Here. Under "B".'

Augusta glanced back at the man in the black coat. He met her gaze and gave a smile before pulling out a book on Gothic architecture.

'*Wuthering Heights*,' said the Irishwoman. 'What's that about?'

'It's set on the Yorkshire moors. But I won't say much more as it might spoil the story for you. I think it's fun to begin a book without knowing too much about it. Then you're in for a nice surprise.'

'Or a disappointment if it turns out to be boring.'

'You won't be disappointed with *Wuthering Heights*.'

'Alright then, I shall try it.'

The Irishwoman made her purchase, then left the shop.

Augusta was now alone with the man in the black coat. She retreated behind the counter and hoped her assistant, Fred, would return soon. He had gone to Holborn Library to collect a box of books which needed repairing.

Augusta occupied herself by feeding some seed to Sparky, the canary who perched in his cage on the counter. From the corner of her eye, she watched the man replace a book on the shelf and approach her.

'Mrs Peel?' His voice was quiet and soft.

Her skin prickled. How did he know her name?

'I'm wondering if you have *The Fair Jilt* or *The Amours of Prince Tarquin and Miranda* by Aphra Behn?'

'I'm afraid I don't.'

'Oh, never mind. I already have a copy of her complete works but I like to collect them individually too. It's a delightful shop you have here.'

'Thank you. If I get any of Aphra Behn's work in stock, I can let you know if you leave me your details.'

'That's kind of you.' He glanced around and leant forward on the counter. 'It's not actually the reason I'm here.'

'Oh?' Although the gentleman seemed pleasant, his manner was unusual. Augusta felt unsure what to make of him. She returned his gaze with a determined glance, keen to demonstrate she was in charge in her bookshop.

'I wanted to wait until we were alone.'

'Why?'

'I've heard you're good at finding people,' he said.

'Who did you hear that from?'

'I prefer not to say. I'm wondering if you could help me.'

'Find someone?'

'Yes.'

Augusta recalled the last person she had been asked to find, Catherine Frankland-Russell. She had made the mistake of not doing enough research into the person who had asked her to carry out the work. She had little interest in repeating the error. 'You do realise there are plenty of detective agencies who can do this work for you? I run a bookshop.'

'Yes, I realise that. It's just that I've heard such good things about the work you do.'

'I must insist on you telling me who told you that. Otherwise, I shall refuse to help at all.'

'Very well.' He sighed. 'I have a friend who's a news reporter and he covers the criminal trials at the Old Bailey. He's heard your name mentioned more than once. Apparently Scotland Yard thinks highly of you.'

To Augusta's disappointment, her reputation was becoming more widely known.

'I can pay good money,' he added.

'I'm not interested in money.'

'Really? It's not often you hear that.' He gave another sigh. 'Look. Mrs Peel. I really could do with your help. I really need to find this person, I have some news for him. I've tried writing to him, contacting mutual friends and placing messages in the classified advertisements and so on. But I've had no luck.'

'What do you want to tell him?'

'It's between me and him, I'm afraid.'

'And how do you know him?'

'We're old friends. I haven't seen him since the war.'

'You're sure he survived the war?'

'Oh yes, I know he did. But we've lost contact since then.'

'Is there a possibility he doesn't wish to hear from you?'

He frowned. 'I don't see why not. No.'

'Would he know where to contact you if he wanted to get in touch with you?'

He scratched the side of his head. 'Yes, I think so. He has my address and I haven't moved recently. But it's important I find him.'

Movement at the shop window caught Augusta's eye. A couple was lingering outside, considering whether to come in.

The man followed her gaze and noticed them too. 'I need to talk to you in private and obviously it's rather difficult here,' he said. 'I can explain it much better to you somewhere else. I think that when you hear my reason for searching for my friend, you'll be happy to help. And I'll insist on paying you good money for it, whether you like it or not.'

The bell on the door sounded as the couple stepped inside the shop. The man pulled a pen and notebook out of his pocket, scribbled something on a page, then tore it out and pushed it across the counter to Augusta. 'My name's Symes,' he said, turning to leave. 'I hope to see you again soon.'

Chapter 2

'"Six o'clock, Thursday, Westminster Abbey cloisters",' said Fred, reading out the note which Symes had given Augusta. She had just explained the strange encounter to him. 'Who is this man?'

'Symes.'

'Who's he?'

'Your guess is as good as mine.'

'Very odd.' Fred adjusted his spectacles and examined the note again. He was a dark-skinned young man who always wore a smart tweed suit. 'A clergyman?' he said. 'Is that why he's suggesting the abbey?'

'He didn't look like a clergyman.'

'It's an unusual meeting place.'

'He's an unusual man. He asked if we have any works by Aphra Behn.'

'The seventeenth century playwright?'

'Yes, that's her. But she's not a well-known writer these days, is she?'

'Not really.'

'Please can you take the box into the workshop? I'm

impatient to see the books you've collected from Holborn Library.'

Fred picked up the cardboard box he'd placed on the floor and carried it through the door behind the counter. Augusta followed him into the workshop where he placed the box on the workbench. Augusta picked up a small knife she used for her book repairs and began cutting the string which the box had been tied up with.

'What did Symes look like?' asked Fred.

'Dark hair which reached his collar. Moustache. Black coat. A little bit taller than me.'

'How old?'

'About twenty-five.'

'I don't remember seeing him.'

'Why would you?'

'He could have visited the shop before.'

'I suppose he could have. I don't think I've seen him in here before either.'

'I wonder what he wants to tell his friend.'

'I wonder that, too. He wouldn't enlighten me.'

'And does the friend want to be found?'

'He might not wish to be. I've made the mistake before of finding someone who didn't want to be found.'

'I remember,' said Fred. 'You don't want to be caught up in something like that again. I take it you're going to ignore this request?'

'It would be sensible to.'

'Good.'

'But…'

'But what?'

'But it would be interesting to find out more.'

Augusta opened the box and was met with the comforting scent of secondhand books. It was a worn paper smell, slightly musty, with a hint of coffee.

'So you're going to meet this Symes character?' asked Fred. 'You don't know anything about him. He could harm you!'

'In Westminster Abbey? I can't imagine it. And I'm sure he doesn't wish to harm me.'

'It might be a trap.'

'You have an active imagination! Why would someone want to set a trap for me?'

'I don't know. But you don't know who you're dealing with, Mrs Peel. Maybe Symes won't be alone when you meet him.'

'I'm sure that if he wanted to cause trouble, then he would suggest a more secluded meeting place.' She began laying the books out on the table. The library considered them too worn and tired to be loaned to readers, so Augusta had bought them, hoping to repair them and sell them in her shop.

'If Symes suggested somewhere secluded, then there's a chance you wouldn't go,' said Fred. 'The cloisters of Westminster Abbey sound safe, but who knows what he's planning?'

'I'll admit to you he made me feel uneasy when he was hanging about in the shop, waiting for me to finish serving a customer. But when he explained that he'd been waiting to speak to me in private, then his behaviour made sense. And besides, he doesn't look the type to harm someone. He seems quite harmless.'

'You seem to be talking yourself into it.'

Augusta thought for a moment. 'Yes, I suppose I am.'

'So I have a suggestion.'

'Which is what?'

'That I come with you.'

'I don't want to take up your evening, Fred.'

'It would give me peace of mind and hopefully help

you, too. I don't have to actually be with you. I could loiter in the background somewhere, just in case there's any trouble.'

'It's a good idea, but only if you really have nothing else to do, Fred.'

'There's not much to do on a late winter evening, is there?' He smiled. 'And the more I think about it, the more intrigued I am to find out what this is all about.'

'It's probably nothing interesting at all,' said Augusta. 'I think we should both prepare to be underwhelmed.'

Chapter 3

'Alfred!' Sylvia grinned broadly as she opened the door to him. Then she lowered her voice to a whisper. 'I feel so nervous!'

'Don't be,' he said, leaning in to kiss her flushed cheek. She smelt of her familiar perfume, lily-of-the-valley. He thought she looked pretty in her tulip pink, low-waisted dress with a large bow at the neckline.

'Come inside,' she said. 'I don't want to let the cold in.'

It was just after five o'clock and dusk was falling. Alfred had watched the sun dip below the rooftops as he had walked from Balham railway station.

In the hallway, strains of Elgar drifted from the gramophone in Sylvia's father's study. Sylvia took Alfred's coat and hung it on the coat stand. Then she lingered for a moment, smoothing her dress and patting her blonde hair into place. 'Are you ready?' she whispered.

His stomach felt knotted. 'I don't think I am.'

She smiled, took his hand, and gave it a firm squeeze. 'I'm sure they're going to be very thrilled.'

'Do you think so? I don't think your father likes me.'

'Oh nonsense! Of course he likes you. He's gruff with everyone. And he wants to protect me. He was just the same with my older sisters and now he gets on with their husbands wonderfully. You've seen how he is with them.'

Alfred recalled the Golding family gathering at Christmas, and how Sylvia's father had joked with his sons-in-law, yet had been dismissive of Alfred. Sylvia had reassured him her father had meant nothing by it, but Alfred didn't feel so sure.

There was a possibility he was worrying too much about Mr Golding's gruff nature. He took in a calming breath and reminded himself it was normal to be concerned that his future father-in-law didn't like him.

He followed Sylvia into the front room which was warmed by the lively blaze in the fireplace. Mrs Golding greeted him with a smile, she was always friendlier than her husband. Belle, the old family spaniel, got up from her resting place on the hearthrug and requested a pat on the head. Her tail wagged happily as Alfred obliged.

'Father will join us shortly,' said Mrs Golding. She had curled silver hair and wore a burgundy dress with a string of pearls. 'He's just catching up on some correspondence.'

The mention of Mr Golding made Alfred's stomach knot again. Sylvia had told him he had to speak to her father before dinner. Then the difficult part would be out of the way, and they could celebrate the happy news as they dined.

Alfred and Sylvia sat stiffly side-by-side on the sofa as Mrs Golding asked Alfred about his day.

'You managed to finish in good time, then?'

'Yes, I asked permission to leave a little earlier. I'll work some extra hours tomorrow to compensate for it.'

'During our walk in the park at the weekend, Alfred was telling me all about diseases of the lung!' said Sylvia.

'Only a little,' he said. 'Not enough to bore you, I hope.'

'No, you didn't bore me at all! It's quite fascinating. Perhaps you can tell Mother and Father at dinner.'

'It's not a suitable subject for mealtime, Sylvia,' said Mrs Golding. 'But no doubt it's fascinating. How long will it be before you're a properly qualified doctor, Alfred?'

'Another three years.'

'It takes a long time, doesn't it? I suppose we should all be reassured by that, though.' She gave a laugh. 'No one wants to be treated by a doctor without the proper training!'

A maid served them with drinks and they talked some more while Alfred kept his eye on the mantelpiece clock. He had to speak to Mr Golding soon, but he felt comfortably rooted to the sofa.

'Gosh, it's already six o'clock,' said Sylvia pointedly. She gave him a sidelong glance, and he knew this was his cue to speak to her father.

He gulped down his sherry, then glanced down at Belle, who was resting her head on one of his feet. Sylvia placed her hand on his and gave it a sharp squeeze. There was no affection in it, just urgency. He winced as the bones of his fingers crunched together.

'Mrs Golding,' he said.

She startled at this sudden announcement. 'Yes, Alfred?'

'May I be permitted to speak with Mr Golding before dinner?'

'Of course. He's in his study. You know where it is, don't you?'

'Yes.'

He pulled his hand away from Sylvia and carefully

retracted his foot from beneath Belle's chin. Then he got to his feet and realised how weak his legs felt.

Sylvia looked up at him, her eyes wide and sparkling with expectation.

He took a deep breath and left the room.

Chapter 4

BELLE FOLLOWED Alfred to the study. The theme from Elgar's *Enigma Variations* grew louder as they walked. Its slow, moody melody instilled a sense of foreboding in Alfred. Did he really love Sylvia enough to put himself through this?

His head felt light and dizzy as he knocked on the door. He had to knock harder a second time to be heard above the music.

'Come in!' The gramophone was turned off. Alfred's sweaty hand slipped on the doorknob as he turned it. He glanced down at Belle for reassurance, then stepped inside.

The room smelt of tobacco and was furnished in dark wood with shelves of books. Mr Golding sat at his desk writing, an empty glass at his elbow. 'Oh, it's you, Smith.' He glanced up, then resumed his work. His preoccupation was an odd pretence, considering he had just taken time to turn off the gramophone. 'What can I do for you?' He was a broad, balding man with hooded eyes and a thick moustache. His shirt sleeves were rolled up and his jacket hung on the back of his chair.

He didn't invite Alfred to sit, so he remained where he was on the rug in front of the desk. Belle trotted over to the fireplace. Alfred cleared his throat and Mr Golding glanced at him again, as if he had forgotten he was there. 'Everything alright, Smith?'

'Everything is alright, sir,' he said. 'I wonder if I may speak with you a moment.'

'That's why you're here, isn't it?'

He felt his face flush warm. Mr Golding had an imperious manner which made him nervous. He wondered if it was intentional. Or was it his own sense of inadequacy which made him feel like this?

Mr Golding lay down his pen and sat back in his chair. 'Would a drink help?'

It was a comforting thought, and he nodded enthusiastically. 'Yes, please.'

Mr Golding picked up his empty glass, got to his feet and marched over to a polished walnut table with a glass decanter and several glasses sitting on a silver tray. He placed his own glass on the tray, picked up a new one, filled it from the decanter and passed the amber drink to Alfred. Then he filled his own glass and turned to face Alfred, one hand in his pocket.

They both took a gulp and Alfred suppressed a gasp from the burn of whisky in his throat.

Mr Golding returned to the chair behind his desk. 'Now you've got a bit of Dutch courage inside you, perhaps you'd like to tell me why you're here?'

Alfred stammered out the words he had planned. 'I would like to ask for your daughter's hand in marriage, Mr Golding.'

A pause followed. Mr Golding picked up a cigar from his desk and examined it.

Alfred wanted to fill the silence with words, but he had

to keep quiet. He had asked the question and needed to wait for the answer.

Mr Golding laid down the cigar and picked up his drink. 'Remind me how old you are, Smith.'

'Twenty-seven.'

'Not particularly young for a bachelor, but we can't ignore the fact the best years of your youth were served in France. As has been the case for most men of your generation. You're a medical student.'

'Yes.'

'So you have no income.'

'I expect a good income once I have qualified as a doctor, sir.'

He nodded. 'Savings?'

'About two hundred pounds.'

'And presumably you'll need to dip into your savings while you finish your studies?'

'I hope not to.'

Mr Golding's moustache bristled as he pondered this. Then he picked up the cigar again and tapped it against his chin.

'I'll be honest with you, Smith,' he said eventually. 'I don't believe you'll make my daughter a good husband.'

Mr Golding didn't like him. Alfred had been right about him all along. He should have ignored Sylvia's assurances and trusted his instincts. And now he was in the shameful position of being turned down.

Alfred took another gulp of whisky and found some words. 'Is there a… particular reason why?'

Mr Golding leaned forward on his desk. 'I don't believe you're husband material, Smith.'

'Are you able to give me an example, sir?'

'Put quite frankly, I believe my daughter can do better. I'm impressed by your war record. It can't have been easy for a man like you in the trenches. By all accounts, you fought with bravery and honour. But when it comes to marrying my daughter… I'm afraid I can't allow it.'

'But Sylvia and I are in love.'

'I'm sure the affliction will pass before long. Sylvia is my youngest daughter. She's only twenty-two and rather naïve. I fear she's fallen for your pretty face but has little idea of what you're really like.'

'I am who I say I am, sir. I'm working extremely hard in my studies and doing well. In a few years' time, I will be a qualified doctor with a good income. I know I can provide for your daughter and make her happy. And I know she will make me very happy too.'

Mr Golding gave a snort. 'Not from what I've heard.'

Alfred felt a cold shiver run through him. What had he heard? Alfred dared not ask.

'You're not really a man of substance,' added Mr Golding. His eyes bore into him and Alfred felt as though he could read every thought of his.

He felt vulnerable and exposed. Almost naked.

He stepped forward and placed his half-empty glass on the desk. As he did so, he noticed his hand trembling.

'In which case, I bid you good evening, sir.'

Mr Golding's eyes remained on him. 'That's it?' He gave a bemused smile. 'I thought you had more fight in you, Smith. But perhaps you know when you're beaten.'

Anger forced him to respond. 'What do you want me to do? Get down on my knees and beg? You've clearly made your mind up about me and have no consideration for your daughter's wishes at all.'

Mr Golding got to his feet. 'I'm protecting her!' he bellowed.

'But if you really cared about her, you'd allow her to follow her heart.'

He turned and left the room, not wishing to be caught up in any further confrontation.

He marched back to the hallway, tears burning his eyes.

As he took his coat from the coat stand, he paused for a moment and wondered if he should return to Sylvia and her mother.

But he couldn't face them.

He flung open the front door and stepped out into the night.

Chapter 5

On Thursday evening, Augusta and Fred travelled by bus through Bloomsbury, the Strand and Whitehall. The clock on Big Ben showed the time was five minutes to six as they disembarked in Westminster.

It was rush hour and the dark, rainy streets were busy with people keen to get home. Augusta and Fred made their way beneath umbrellas through Parliament Square. To their left, lights glimmered from the mullioned windows of the Palace of Westminster. A short walk beyond the building brought them to the towering form of Westminster Abbey. Its tall, arched windows were warmly lit and Augusta looked forward to getting out of the rain.

Inside the abbey, they stood in awe of the vast vaulted ceiling which reached high above their heads. Rainwater dripped from their coats and folded umbrellas onto the tiled floor. There were a few other people inside. Some sauntered slowly, taking in the scale of the place, while others sat in quiet contemplation.

'I wonder why Symes suggested this place?' said

Augusta. Despite the size of the abbey, she felt the need to whisper in its hushed, echoing interior.

'Perhaps he'll explain when you meet him,' said Fred.

'I hope so. It's all very mysterious. Which is why we're here, I suppose.'

Two rows of thick stone columns flanked the nave and led to an elaborate screen with an altar in front of it. From previous visits here, Augusta knew there was another nave and altar beyond the screen. The abbey was enormous. And almost a thousand years old.

'Cloisters,' said Augusta, pointing to a little wooden sign attached to a column. 'We need to turn right.'

A heavy wooden door, worn smooth with age, opened out into a covered walkway which ran around a square of grass. Dim lights were set on the walls alongside ornate memorials. A low stone bench ran along each wall, providing a seat for rest and reflection. Rain pattered on the grass, but the stone vaulted roof kept Augusta and Fred dry.

'It feels like a monastery here,' said Fred.

'It's so quiet, isn't it? It's easy to forget we're in the centre of London.'

'And there's hardly anyone about.'

'Where's Symes?'

They proceeded along the worn stone flags and Augusta thought of the countless feet which had walked here over the centuries. Tombstones were inlaid in the paving. Some looked modern and others were so old that their inscriptions were barely legible.

Fred checked his watch. 'It's ten past six now, we're a little late. Do you think he'll still be here?'

'I hope so. Let's walk around until we see him. Wait…' Augusta's eye was drawn to a man sitting on the stone bench. 'Is that him?'

'If it is, then it looks like he's nodded off!'

They walked towards the seated figure, who wore a long dark coat and a bowler hat. As they drew nearer, Augusta could see his head was slumped with his chin on his left shoulder. His overcoat was undone, as was his jacket beneath it. His waistcoat and trousers were black.

'That's a deep sleep,' said Fred as they stood in front of him.

'Mr Symes?' said Augusta.

There was no answer.

She turned to Fred. 'Do you think he's alright?'

'No, I don't,' said Fred, stooping to inspect the gentleman. 'Hello, Mr Symes?' He waited for a moment, then turned back to Augusta. 'He must be unwell.'

'Very unwell.' Augusta's heart began to thud.

Something was wrong.

'I think I saw him breathe just then,' said Fred. 'I'll feel for a pulse.' He knelt by Mr Symes, pulled up his coat sleeve, and rested a finger on the inside of his wrist. 'It could be drink,' he added. 'But I can't smell drink.'

'Wait.' Although the waistcoat was black, Augusta could see a dark patch on it. A stain of some sort. She leaned forward and pulled open one side of his overcoat.

Then her head felt dizzy with a wave of nausea.

'Blood,' she said.

'Where?'

'Here.' She moved the coat some more to reveal the dark, damp stain spreading across Mr Symes's clothing. She lifted part of his waistcoat and saw his shirt beneath was stained bright red.

'Oh, good grief!' Fred jumped to his feet. 'We need to get help! I think he's alive. I'm sure I felt a faint pulse.'

'Hopefully we can save him.' Augusta took off her scarf. 'I'll try to staunch the wound with this. You go and tell someone. We need a doctor!'

Chapter 6

'I SHALL SUMMARISE what you've just told me, Mrs Peel,' said the police sergeant. 'A gentleman walked into your Bloomsbury bookshop on Monday afternoon and asked you to help him find a long-lost friend.'

'Yes.'

'Then he arranged to meet you in the cloisters of Westminster Abbey at six o'clock this evening.'

'That's right.'

'Did you not think it strange?'

'I thought it was very strange, which is why I agreed to the meeting.'

Sergeant Wilcox sighed and examined his notebook. Augusta and Fred were sitting with him in an austere interview room in Rochester Row police station. After they had raised the alarm in Westminster Abbey, a doctor had been called. Mr Symes had been taken by ambulance to St Thomas's Hospital which faced the Houses of Parliament on the south bank of the River Thames.

'Did you see anyone else in the cloisters?' asked the sergeant.

'No.'

'So someone attacked this gentleman before you found him, then escaped without being seen.'

'They must have done.'

'Or they hid,' said Fred.

'Hid?' asked the sergeant. 'Where?'

'I don't know. Maybe they jumped over the wall and onto the grass and hid there.'

'Did you look there?'

'No, we didn't look anywhere,' said Augusta. 'Our priority was to help Mr Symes.'

'Someone had just attacked him and you didn't think to search for them?'

'No. I just assumed they'd got away. There were a few doors nearby. I don't know where they led to. I suppose the attacker could've escaped through any one of them. We just tried to help Mr Symes. If we'd been any later, he might have succumbed to his injuries.'

The sergeant sat back in his chair and rested his palms on the back of his head. He stared at Fred as if trying to make up his mind about him. Then he spoke again, 'Your story makes little sense, Mrs Peel. Why would a complete stranger visit your shop with a vague request which he's reluctant to tell you more about until he meets you in Westminster Abbey?'

'I don't know. He wrote the meeting place on a piece of paper.'

'And where is that piece of paper now?'

'In my shop. I can give it to you tomorrow.'

'Yes, I should like to see it. You do realise his name is not Mr Symes?'

'No. What's his name?'

'Robert Trigwell. We found a club membership card in his wallet.'

'His name wasn't Symes?' This new piece of information felt dizzying.

'No. Where did you get Symes from?'

'That's what he told me his name was.'

'When he visited your shop?'

'Yes.'

'Are you sure you heard him properly?'

'Quite sure.'

'I don't think I've ever come across a case as peculiar as this.'

'Me neither.'

The sergeant released his hands from behind his head and leant forward, resting his elbows on the table. 'And what's to say the pair of you haven't made this story up?'

'Why would we do that?' asked Augusta.

'Because you attacked him.'

'But we didn't!'

'Perhaps you didn't, Mrs Peel. But what about your friend here?'

He gave Fred another stare. Augusta suspected that Fred's dark skin colour was prompting the police officer to suspect him of wrongdoing.

'Fred helps me run my bookshop,' she said to the sergeant. 'You can't possibly suspect him of any criminal activity.'

'But he's a foreigner.'

'No I'm not,' said Fred. 'I was born in Lewisham.'

'He's lived in London for his entire life,' added Augusta. 'Longer than me, in fact. Now if the pair of us had attacked Mr Trigwell, then surely we'd have run off and left him to die?'

'Perhaps. Perhaps not. Can you see my dilemma, Mrs Peel? A man is attacked in the cloisters of Westminster Abbey and there are no witnesses. Then two people who claim to have found him tell me a strange tale of how he'd visited their shop a few days previously and asked them to find a long-lost friend. It doesn't sound plausible.'

'No, it doesn't. But it's what happened.'

'Did he tell you the name of the long-lost friend?'

'No.'

'How convenient.'

Augusta felt a twinge of anger. 'This isn't about convenience, Sergeant, this is about the truth! I'm telling you everything that happened.'

'But you didn't even have the right name.'

'I used the name he gave me!'

'Very well. I can't help thinking there's something very fishy about this.'

'Will you be getting Scotland Yard involved?'

'No, I don't see any need for that. Not unless the chap dies, and it becomes a murder case.'

'I think Detective Inspector Fisher will do a good job of working this one out,' said Augusta.

'Do you? And what makes you say that?'

'He's a good detective. And a friend.'

The sergeant regarded her for a moment, his lips pursed. 'So you think your friend will get you out of this? Is that why you're mentioning him?'

'There's nothing for me to get out of, Sergeant. I've done nothing wrong.'

Chapter 7

'Sparky, mind your manners!' scolded Lady Hereford.
'You mustn't snatch the seed from me, you must take it
carefully. I think this canary needs a little more discipline,
Augusta, I hope you're not being soft with him.'

The old lady sat in her bath chair by the counter in
Augusta's bookshop. She had neatly waved white hair and
wore a velvet coat trimmed with fur. Her eyes were a
striking blue, and pink circles of rouge sat high on her
cheeks.

'Is it possible to discipline a canary?' asked Augusta
with a smile.

'Oh yes, it's all in the tone of voice.'

Sparky belonged to Lady Hereford, but Augusta looked
after him. Lady Hereford felt the bookshop was a more
interesting environment for the bird than her quiet rooms
in the nearby Russell Hotel.

'I don't like the idea of raising my voice at Sparky,' said
Augusta.

'You don't need to raise your voice. Just a firm instruc-
tional tone is all that's needed. Isn't that right, Sparky?'

The canary snatched another seed from her and Lady Hereford tutted. 'Now he's just being naughty on purpose.' She handed the bag of birdseed to Augusta. 'He can have some more once he behaves himself. Now tell me what you've been up to.'

'Fred and I found an injured man in Westminster Abbey yesterday evening.'

Lady Hereford's mouth dropped open. 'You found him? I read all about it in the newspaper this morning, but I had no idea you were there.'

Augusta explained how she had become involved.

'Goodness,' said the old lady once she had finished. 'Let's hope he makes a recovery. And to think that something so awful could happen in a house of God! Just dreadful. It makes you wonder what the world is coming to. Oh, and while I remember, there's something I need to tell you. I had dinner with Sir Pritchard at the weekend.'

Augusta had never met Sir Pritchard, but he was Lady Hereford's friend and the landlord of Augusta's bookshop.

'He informed me there's a new tenant moving into the rooms above this shop. He told me to let you know.'

Augusta had given little thought to the rooms above her shop before. 'Is it a flat or offices up there?' she asked.

'Offices. And a bookkeeping company is moving in. Apparently, they were in some offices in the City which are too expensive for them. You'd think a bookkeeping firm would know how to keep on top of its costs, wouldn't you? Anyway, you're going to have some people upstairs.'

'I'm not sure I want any people upstairs.'

Lady Hereford laughed. 'I'm sure they'll be absolutely fine. And it must be preferable to having empty rooms above you. There's something about empty rooms which is quite creepy, don't you think?' The bell on the shop door rang. 'It looks like you have a customer. Oh no, it's not. It's your police inspector friend!'

Detective Inspector Philip Fisher entered the shop, leaning on his walking stick for support. He wore an overcoat and bowler hat. A few weeks had passed since Augusta had last seen him, and his face seemed a little thinner. As he smiled, the crow's feet at his eyes looked deeper.

'Philip!' She grinned. 'How have you been keeping?'

'Well. Thank you, Augusta. Good morning, Lady Hereford.' He removed his hat. 'How are you both? And Fred!'

Fred had appeared from the door behind the counter. 'Hello, Detective Inspector Fisher.'

'I've heard all about you and Augusta in Westminster Abbey.'

Fred shook his head. 'Awful.'

'I take it Sergeant Wilcox has spoken to you, Philip?' asked Augusta.

'Yes, he telephoned me this morning and wanted to know if you and Fred are the sort of people who stab strangers in cathedral cloisters.'

'And what did you tell him?'

'I told him there was no doubt about it.'

'Oh dear.'

'I'm sorry, that was a poor joke. I assured Sergeant Wilcox that I've known you a long time and there wasn't the slightest possibility that you and Fred would have attacked that gentleman.'

'Thank you, Philip. I've been worrying he didn't believe us.'

'Thank you for your help, Detective Inspector Fisher,' added Fred. 'I was worried Sergeant Wilcox had it in for me.'

'Hopefully he'll leave you alone now. And it's about time you called me Philip. We've known each other for long enough. I suppose Sergeant Wilcox struggled to believe you because he's baffled by the story.'

'And so are we,' said Augusta. 'I don't understand why Mr Trigwell told me his name was Symes. And it's odd he came in here on Monday to purposefully seek me out.'

'How did he know about you?' asked Philip.

'He told me a friend of his was a reporter and had heard my name mentioned in a trial. I've no idea who his friend is.'

'With a bit of luck, we can find out more as he recovers.'

'Word is clearly spreading about you, Augusta,' said Lady Hereford.

'I don't want it to.'

'Why not?'

'Because I'd rather repair and sell books.'

'But you went to the abbey to meet this fellow,' said Philip. 'So that suggests you had some interest in carrying out his request.'

'Yes…' said Augusta, a little embarrassed at being caught out. 'I suppose I was interested. It's because it all seemed quite mysterious.'

'And it's become even more mysterious now he's been attacked. However, the important thing is that Sergeant Wilcox doesn't treat you and Fred as suspects. He needs to put his energies into finding the attacker. I'm sure some witnesses can be found. Someone must have seen the attacker making a getaway. I'm hoping they'll find the knife, too. It could have some useful fingerprints on it.'

'Perhaps we'll find out the identity of Mr Trigwell's long-lost friend,' said Augusta. 'I'll visit the hospital this afternoon and hopefully he'll be well enough to talk to.'

'Perhaps the long-lost friend has heard about the attack and is by his bedside?' said Lady Hereford. 'It could all be resolved with a happy ending.'

'That's a nice thought,' said Philip. 'I like happy endings.'

'So do I,' said Augusta.

But she suspected this case would not be as straightforward as that.

Chapter 8

THAT AFTERNOON, Augusta took the bus to Westminster then walked across Westminster Bridge. From the bridge, she could see St Thomas's Hospital stretching along the south bank of the river. It was a vast place, comprising seven, four-storey buildings. Augusta recalled reading that the famed nurse, Florence Nightingale, had helped with the design of the hospital to ensure the wards were well lit and ventilated.

Augusta had little doubt the hospital was well ventilated today. The icy wind on the bridge was so strong that she had to lean into it and hold on to her hat as she walked.

A porter at the hospital reception desk told Augusta which block and ward she could find Robert Trigwell on. His directions sent her on a long walk through a shiny-floored corridor which smelled of boiled cabbage mixed with disinfectant. Doctors, nurses and orderlies with trolleys jostled for space with the other hospital visitors.

Eventually, Augusta found a staircase which led to the ward. At the door, she introduced herself to a glum-faced nurse. 'I would like to visit Mr Trigwell, please. I found him injured yesterday evening. How is he faring?'

The nurse sighed. 'I'm afraid he's just passed away.'

Augusta stared at her for a moment, trying to accustom herself to this news. 'He's died? When?'

The nurse checked the watch pinned to her stiff white apron. 'About half an hour ago.'

'Is that all?' Augusta shook her head. 'I was hoping to speak to him.'

'He was unconscious for most of his time here. He was very seriously injured. The police were here this morning wanting to speak to him too, but he wouldn't stir. We had to ask them to leave because we were worried they were affecting his recovery. We had some hope he might find the strength to get better. But sadly, it wasn't to be.'

'Did he say anything about what had happened to him?'

'No. All we could do was make him as comfortable as possible.'

'So he didn't say anything at all?'

'I'll fetch Nurse Drew. She was the one who spent the most time with him.'

As she waited for Nurse Drew, Augusta struggled to contain her sadness. She had barely known Mr Trigwell, but she found this news upsetting. Who could have attacked him in such a cruel way? And in such a peaceful place?

Nurse Drew had a freckled face and looked no older than twenty.

'He was too unwell to speak much,' she said. 'But he woke a little after the police left and tried to say something. He was too weak to make much sense.'

'But did you understand anything he said?'

'Yes. He kept trying to say a name. He said it four or five times and I finally understood it. I thought I should make a note of it.'

'You've written it down?'

'Yes.' She pulled a piece of paper from her apron. 'Alfie Smith.'

'And I don't suppose he explained who Alfie Smith is?'

'No, he was incapable of that.'

'Did he say anything else?'

'Just a number.'

'A telephone number?'

'I don't know. I wrote it down because it seemed important to him. I don't suppose the number means anything to you?' She showed it to Augusta. It was comprised of five digits: 78341.

'I'm afraid it means nothing to me,' she said. 'Do you mind if I copy it down?'

'Not at all.'

Augusta took her notebook and pen from her handbag and copied out the number. 'And Alfie Smith, you say?'

'Yes.'

'The name of the person who attacked him, perhaps?'

'I don't know.'

'Please can you tell the police this information?'

'Of course. I'll telephone them now.'

'And how did Robert Trigwell seem when he spoke? Angry?'

'No, not angry. He was much too weak for that. He mumbled it. I asked him who Alfie was, but he was unable to give me a response. And then he repeated the number and fell asleep.'

'Did he wake again before he died?'

'Sadly he didn't.'

'Has anyone visited him since he arrived here?'

'No, only the police.'

'No family or friends?'

Nurse Drew shook her head.

'Thank you. You've been extremely helpful.'

'I wish I could have done more.'

'I'm sure you did everything you could. Someone clearly wished to end his life and sadly, they've been successful.'

Chapter 9

As she left St Thomas's Hospital, Augusta knew she had to speak to Philip. The attack on Robert Trigwell was now a murder case, and she felt sure Scotland Yard would be involved. As luck would have it, the buildings of New Scotland Yard were just a short walk back over the river.

Philip was speaking to a young gentleman when she arrived in his wood-panelled office.

'Augusta!' he said with a smile. 'Meet our new recruit, Detective Sergeant Joyce.'

The detective shook her hand. He had fair, side-parted hair and a boyish face. A sparse moustache ran along his top lip and Augusta wondered if he was growing it to make himself look older.

'This is Augusta Peel,' Philip explained to him. 'We worked together in intelligence during the war.'

'How interesting,' said Detective Sergeant Joyce. 'You're one of these lady detectives now, are you, Mrs Peel?'

'No. I'm a bookseller.'

'Oh.'

'But I sometimes help Detective Inspector Fisher with his cases.'

'Two minds are better than one,' said Philip.

'Absolutely. Well, it's a pleasure to meet you Mrs Peel.' He turned to Philip. 'Thank you for explaining your new case to me. I shall leave you to it for the time being.'

'Cheerio.'

Philip's smile faded once Detective Sergeant Joyce had left the room.

'You don't like him?' whispered Augusta.

'There's nothing wrong with *him*,' said Philip. 'But he's the commissioner's son. He joined the Metropolitan Police as a constable less than three years ago! He's got very little experience for a detective of his rank. But I don't suppose that matters when you're the commissioner's son.'

'He's going to find the work very difficult with such limited experience.'

'He is. But I don't suppose that's my problem. His father can deal with that. Did you manage to speak to Robert Trigwell before he died?'

'Sadly not. You heard about his death quickly.'

'Sergeant Wilcox telephoned me,' said Philip. 'The hospital telephoned him as soon as the poor chap passed away. So it's a murder investigation now.'

'And his murderer could be called Alfie Smith,' said Augusta.

'Yes, Wilcox told me about the information the nurse got from him.'

'Alfie could also be Alfred.'

'Yes. And I should think there are a fair few Alfred Smiths about. We need to find one who knew Robert Trigwell.'

'I don't understand the number he gave the nurse.' Augusta pulled out her notebook. 'I've written it down here.'

Philip put on his reading glasses and examined the number. 'Five digits. What can it mean? One digit longer than a telephone number. Unless you include the number for the exchange. But that's three digits which would give you seven digits overall. This is only five.'

'Could it be a meaningful date?'

'78341. I doubt it. Perhaps it's a code? Let's think about some of those ciphers we used in Belgium during the war.'

'The simplest one would be the Caesar cipher.'

Philip sat down at his desk and gestured for Augusta to pull up a chair and join him. He opened his notebook and picked up a pen.

'Let's try the Caesar cipher,' he said. 'What's the first number you've written down? Seven. So the seventh letter in the alphabet is G.' He wrote this down. 'Then the other numbers correlate to H... C... D... and A. That doesn't look promising, does it? You can't even make an anagram from it.'

'Could it stand for something?'

They both stared at the collection of letters for a moment, but nothing came to mind.

'Baravelli's code?' said Philip.

'It could be. But we'd need the codebook to get any further with it.'

'What about the ADFGVX code?'

'But if it's a codeword, then it's very short. If each number represents a letter, then it can only be one or two words long,' said Augusta.

'Good point. Perhaps each number represents a word?

Just like you find in book cipher. But there's little chance of solving that without the key text for the code.'

'Perhaps there's something in Mr Trigwell's home which could help?'

'A codebook or document with the key text! Yes, that's possible. I'll ask Sergeant Wilcox to make sure his men look for something like that.'

'Coded messages are usually longer than this,' said Augusta. 'In fact, I've never seen one this short before. Let's try something else. What do the numbers add up to? Twenty-three.'

'What could that mean?'

'I don't know.'

'Perhaps the numbers are coordinates? Seventy-eight degrees latitude… but we can't have three hundred and forty-one longitude because the maximum is one hundred and eighty. Seventy-three latitude and thirty-four longitude?'

'What about the number one at the end?'

'I'll ignore that for now.' Philip chewed the end of his pen. 'Let's think about these coordinates for a moment. Seventy-three degrees latitude puts you some distance north of here. Close to the Arctic, I'd say. And I think thirty-four longitude is probably near Moscow and runs south from there through the Middle East. So I think those coordinates would be a place in… the middle of the Barents Sea.'

'It's possible we're reading too much into this,' said Augusta.

Philip smiled. 'I think you could be right. Perhaps I'm getting a little carried away.'

'Perhaps it's a sum of money?'

'Over seventy-eight thousand pounds? That's a lot of money.'

'Perhaps it's a bank account number?'

'Fairly useless if we don't know which bank it's with.'

'Perhaps Sergeant Wilcox and his men will find something in Mr Trigwell's home which could help? I don't think it's worth spending any more time now trying to read sense into this number. We may get another clue.'

'You're right, Augusta. We need to search his home, speak to his friends and family and find out what he did for a living, too. Hopefully, we'll be a lot wiser soon enough. And we're already making good progress. Sergeant Wilcox also told me on the telephone that the murder weapon has been recovered from Westminster Abbey.'

'That's excellent news! Where was it found?'

'On the square of grass in the middle of the cloisters. The murderer must have thrown it over the wall before running away. It's being dusted for fingerprints as we speak.'

Chapter 10

'I THINK it's very sad Robert Trigwell has died,' said Fred to Augusta the following Monday. 'And if we hadn't been late to meet him, his attacker may never have struck!'

'I know,' said Augusta. 'I keep thinking the same. But we couldn't have foreseen what happened. Nor can we change it now. And even if we had prevented the attack that evening, I suspect his killer would have caught up with him another time.'

'I wonder why they wanted him dead?'

'Me too. Hopefully Philip and his men have learned some more about him now. The clues will come from family, friends and associates. And perhaps his home, too.' Augusta checked her watch. 'It's nearly ten o'clock. I'd better get started on repairing those books you brought back from Holborn Library. The sooner they're on the shelves, the sooner we can sell them.'

A noise from the mezzanine floor above their heads interrupted them.

'I didn't realise there was a customer in the shop, did you, Fred?'

'No.'

They listened as someone descended the staircase. It was a man in a dark overcoat. He didn't look around the rest of the shop, instead he headed straight for the door and left.

'I didn't even notice him come in,' said Fred. 'And I don't like the way he swiftly left like that. It makes you wonder if he hid a book or two under his coat.'

'I hope not!'

Augusta dashed up the stairs and began scouring the shelves for any sign of missing books. It was going to be difficult to establish whether the man had actually taken anything, but she thought it was worth her while looking for any obvious gaps.

Everything looked just as it should. Then Augusta's eyes were drawn to something she had previously given little thought to.

'Maybe he came out of here,' she said.

'From where?' asked Fred from downstairs.

'This door,' she said. It was a plain wooden door in the corner, flanked either side by bookcases. It was the sort of door which was unused and forgotten about. Augusta had assumed it either led to unused storage space or an adjoining property. It had always been locked and she didn't have a key for it. She stepped over to it and tried the handle. 'It's locked,' she said. 'Like it always is.'

Fred had now joined her. 'It must lead to the offices.'

'Do you think the bookkeeper's firm has moved in?'

'Maybe they moved in when we were closed yesterday.'

'Maybe they did. But no one should be using this door. The offices above the shop have their own entrance from the street.'

'This door must be a shortcut.'

'I don't see how. Do you really think the man came out

of here? I think he must have been a customer we hadn't noticed.'

'If he crept in without us noticing, we need to be more vigilant.'

'Definitely! This awful business with Robert Trigwell is distracting us too much, Fred. Let's try to pay attention a little more.'

Chapter 11

Augusta began work on repairing a copy of *Little Dorrit* in her workshop. It was one of the books which Fred had collected from the library and, to her annoyance, she discovered someone had made pencil annotations in the margins. She picked up a piece of pliable rubber and set about carefully lifting the marks from the pages. It was painstaking work, but the book was otherwise in good condition. She considered it time well spent.

While she worked, she heard the telephone ring in the shop. Moments later, Fred appeared at the door. 'Detective Inspector Fisher would like to speak to you,' he said.

'He's got some news?'

'I expect so, but he wants to speak to you.'

Augusta could feel a crick in her neck as she walked to the telephone. She hadn't realised how long she had been stooped over her work.

'Augusta!' Philip sounded pleased. 'I thought I'd let you know what we've found out about this Robert Trigwell character. Sergeant Wilcox and his men at B Division have been searching his flat in Wood Street, just a few streets away from Westminster Abbey. Full name Robert Barnabas Trigwell. Twenty-six years old. Born in Hampstead to Hugo and Margaret Trigwell, both deceased. They seem to have been a respectable middle-class family. Trigwell senior worked in banking and they appear to have lived comfortably in a sizeable house. There's an older sister, Isabella Trigwell, who lives in Chelsea. I understand the mother and daughter lived in a flat together there after the death of Hugo Trigwell a few years ago. Mrs Trigwell died only last month.'

'How sad for the sister!' said Augusta. 'She's lost two family members in just two months.'

'Sad indeed. Robert Trigwell was unmarried and lived alone. He served on the Western Front during the war and after that he found work at the company J Baker.'

'As in Baker's Tea Rooms?'

'That's right. The famous bakery and tearoom company. I must say, I like their iced buns. Robert worked as a senior clerk in the finance department.'

'So any clues yet on why someone would harm him?'

'None, I'm afraid. But I'm going to visit the sister, Isabella Trigwell, tomorrow morning. Would you like to accompany me?'

'Yes, I would.'

'You might want to tell her about Robert's visit to your shop and his request. She may be able to shed some light on it. She might know who Alfie Smith is, too.'

'I hope so.'

Philip lowered his voice a little. 'The new boy, Detective Sergeant Joyce, wants to come along too. He's very keen to get involved with this case.'

'I see.' Augusta didn't like the idea of a third person being involved. She and Philip worked together so well that she could only see Joyce as a hindrance. And with his lack of experience, she wasn't sure how he could help. 'I suppose he has to learn how to manage these cases,' she added, diplomatically.

'Exactly. Now I've been having a think about this murder and I've settled on two possibilities. Mr Trigwell's killer either knew he'd planned to meet you at Westminster Abbey or he followed him there. Let's start with the first possibility. Was there anyone else in the shop when he discussed meeting you there?'

'No. He waited for the other customers to leave before he spoke to me. And besides, he wrote our meeting place on a piece of paper.'

'Did he say it out loud?'

'No, he just wrote it down.'

'Could anyone else have seen what was written on the piece of paper?'

'No. There was no one else there.'

'What did you do with the piece of paper after he gave it to you?'

'I showed it to Fred and then I folded it up and put it on a shelf beneath the counter.'

'So someone else could have found it and read it?'

'Possibly. But I've no idea who. And even if someone had found it, they wouldn't have known what it referred to.'

'Do you still have the note?'

'Yes, I think it's still on the shelf.'

'And remind me of its wording again.'

'I'll fetch it now.' Augusta left the telephone receiver dangling from the wall as she went to fetch the note. It was where she had left it. '"Six o'clock, Thursday, Westminster Abbey cloisters",' she said to Philip once she had returned to the telephone.

'As you say, it would be meaningless to most people.'

'And the note was where I left it,' said Augusta. 'If someone somehow came into the shop and looked behind the counter and read it then they must have left it in exactly the same place. I think it's unlikely.'

'So who did you tell about the note?'

'Fred.'

'Anyone else?'

'No one else.'

'And did Fred mention it to anyone?'

'I don't think so.'

'Can you ask him?'

Augusta looked across the shop to where her assistant was talking to a customer. 'He's with someone at the moment.'

'Fine. Ask him later when you find the chance, then. But let's assume for now he didn't tell anyone else. Were there any customers in the shop while you were discussing it?'

'No, I don't think so.'

'So neither of you mentioned the meeting to anyone else,' said Philip. 'And we're as certain as we can be that no one else saw the note. So that brings me to the second possibility. Mr Trigwell's assailant could have been following him.'

'It's the only other explanation I can think of,' said Augusta. 'Either that or Mr Trigwell was regularly in the cloisters of Westminster Abbey at six o'clock in the evening.'

'Now that's an interesting idea,' said Philip. 'Why would he do that?'

'Your guess is as good as mine.'

Chapter 12

Sylvia sat down at the table in Baker's Tea Rooms on Oxford Street and scowled at Alfred.

'Hello Sylvia.'

'So you turned up then?'

'Of course.'

'And yet you didn't have the courtesy to say goodbye when you left our house last week! It was very rude of you!'

'So you said in your letter.'

She unwrapped her pink woollen scarf and placed it on the back of her chair. 'And when were you planning to write to me? Or telephone? Or call on me?'

'I was going to write, Sylvia, but you beat me to it. And I didn't want to call on you because I don't wish to show my face at your house again.'

'Because my father doesn't approve of our engagement?'

'Yes. And from the way you say it, you make it sound as though it's just a small thing. It isn't!'

'But we don't need his blessing, do we? It's not like the

old days. If we want to get married, then we can do so. My parents can't stop us.'

'But can you imagine how intolerable it would be with them disapproving of me the entire time? Every family gathering would be torture. It would be impossible to celebrate a birthday, anniversary or Christmas without some awful atmosphere. And what about our children? Would your father's disapproval of me extend to them, too?'

'Of course not! And besides, as soon as we have children, I feel quite sure he'll come round.'

'And if he doesn't? I think the daily strain would be unbearable.'

'But if we love each other, then surely nothing else matters?'

He took her hand and smiled. 'I agree, Sylvia. Nothing else matters.' He desperately wanted to marry her, but what if her parents disowned her as a result? 'If we go ahead with marriage, then you could become estranged from your family.'

'Nonsense. They'll get used to the idea.'

He didn't feel so sure. 'Will they?'

'Once they see how happy you make me, then they'll give us their blessing.'

'Really?'

'Oh, you mustn't let Father get to you. You take him too seriously! He can be very grumpy sometimes, but I know he wouldn't want to lose me. If I threatened to choose you over them, then he would come to his senses.'

A waitress arrived at their table and they placed an order for two cups of tea.

Alfred sensed Sylvia wasn't quite so angry with him anymore. He relaxed and took off his coat.

'He may be pleased to see you happy. But he doesn't like me.' He felt the cold sensation in his stomach again as he recalled how Mr Golding had mentioned he had heard stories about him.

'Don't take him too seriously. Perhaps try to have a joke with him sometimes. You can be so terribly sombre sometimes, Alfred.'

He laughed. It felt impossible to humour Mr Golding.

'You mustn't let it hurt your feelings.'

'I don't think you realise what it's like when you're not accepted.'

'Of course you're accepted! I think you're making too much of this now.'

She smiled, and he did his best to share her enthusiasm. She knew her father better than he did. But was she right about him? She couldn't feel the shame and disapproval which he had felt as he stood in Mr Golding's study.

But perhaps he was too serious. And perhaps he worried too much about what other people thought. He had found the girl he wanted to marry and he couldn't allow anything, or anyone, to get in the way of their union.

Chapter 13

AUGUSTA RETURNED to Westminster Abbey that evening. It was the same time of day that Robert Trigwell had been murdered and she hoped that going there would jog her memory about something.

The cloisters were quiet and dimly lit, just as they had been on the evening of the attack. Augusta gave a shiver as she walked towards the place where she and Fred had found Robert Trigwell mortally injured. Had the murderer been close by when she and Fred had discovered him here? She paused and surveyed the square in the centre. The grass was a dull grey colour in the gloom. That was where the knife had been found. Had the murderer thrown the knife there? Or actually hidden there? It surprised her there were no witnesses yet who had seen someone acting suspiciously.

Augusta went on her way and reached the spot where they had found Robert Trigwell. There was no sign that a fatal attack had occurred there. She shuddered as she sat where he had sat. Then she looked up and down the walkway and wondered how his attacker had approached him.

Had he known his killer? It must have initially been a calm encounter because there was no suggestion he had tried to escape the attack. He had remained in the place he had arranged to meet Augusta. Had he fought back? She couldn't recall seeing injuries on his hands.

Augusta felt sure Robert must have known his killer and possibly trusted them, too. They had got close enough to him to plunge a knife into his side without a fight. It had been a cold, calculated attack. It was sickening to think some people were capable of such brutality.

She didn't enjoy sitting here in this cold, quiet place. But she remained for a few moments longer just in case some new thoughts came to her mind. A name on a tombstone inlaid in the floor caught her eye.

Aphra Behn. Where had she heard that name before?

With a startle, Augusta recalled it was the writer which Robert Trigwell had enquired about during his visit to her bookshop. She got to her feet and read the inscription on the tomb:

Mrs Aphra Behn, Dyed April 16 A.D. 1689. Here lies a Proof that Wit can never be Defence enough against Mortality.

Augusta smiled at the last line. She liked the thought that Aphra Behn had been witty, it wasn't a description often used for women. There was a sadness to the inscription too. A suggestion that no strength or brilliance could withstand mortality. It was a reminder of humankind's frailty.

It was obvious now why Robert Trigwell had chosen this place. It had to be a spot he had visited regularly. Had the killer known that he did so?

She hadn't spotted the tomb inscription on her previous visit. She and Fred had been too concerned with helping Robert. She thought of Alfie Smith and wondered if that was a reference to another tomb close by. She looked at the memorials and tombstones nearby but couldn't see the name or anything similar to it.

Robert Trigwell had imparted two pieces of information to the nurse at St Thomas's Hospital. Augusta couldn't imagine what it was like to be close to death, but she felt sure he would only have told the nurse something that really mattered to him.

The first was the name Alfie Smith. It must either be the person who attacked him or the person he had wanted her to find. Perhaps Robert Trigwell's family or friends had heard of him?

And the second piece of information was the number. What did it represent? And why had he gone to so much trouble to recite it?

Chapter 14

THE FOLLOWING MORNING, Augusta waited for Philip outside Sloane Square tube station. She watched the respectable residents of Chelsea pass by: men in smart hats, elegant ladies with shopping bags, and nannies encouraging their young charges to enjoy their morning walk in the cold.

'Sorry I'm late,' said Philip's voice at her shoulder. She turned, and they exchanged a smile. 'Detective Sergeant Joyce is meeting us outside the apartment building. And because I'm late, he'll be hanging about having to wait for us. Never mind. It will teach him some patience. An important skill for a detective.'

Augusta laughed. 'A very important skill.'

Philip pulled a scrap of paper from his overcoat pocket. 'I've drawn a map here, which made sense to me at the time, but looks little more than a scribble now. Sloane Court. Presumably quite close to us here in Sloane Square?'

Augusta peered at his hastily drawn map. 'I think we need to go left.'

'You think so? Alright then, let's give it a go.'

They went on their way, Philip's walking stick tapping on the ground as they walked.

'How have things been?' Augusta asked. Philip's wife had recently left him and she knew he had been finding the change difficult. She was wary of broaching the subject with him because he rarely mentioned anything about it.

'Things are going well. I saw my son at the weekend. I travelled down to Bognor Regis to see him and he remembered me, so that's something.' Philip's son, Michael, was about two years old. 'We had a short walk together along the exceptionally cold seafront. It was blowing a gale down there! I struggle to understand why anyone would wish to be by the British coast out of summertime. But I suppose my estranged wife's parents live there, so that's why Michael's there.'

'It must have been nice to see him.'

'It was. It's a strange situation and I worry I'll become a stranger to him. Seeing him just once a month isn't really enough. I'd like him to stay with me, but my job doesn't make that easy. The work is unpredictable, you never know what's going to come up.'

'Could you employ someone to help?'

'I suppose I could do. But the person would be a stranger to him, wouldn't they? There doesn't seem a point in having him to stay and then being away from him. He's probably better off in Bognor with his mother and grandparents. Oh, there's a sign saying Lower Sloane Street. Do you think we're getting any closer?' They paused by a row of shops and he pulled out the map again. 'We need to look for Turk's Row.'

Once they had established where they needed to go, Augusta told him about her visit to Westminster Abbey the previous evening. 'And I think Robert Trigwell was a regular visitor to the cloisters,' she added.

'What makes you say that?'

'I spotted something I hadn't noticed there before. The place where he was attacked was close to the grave of Aphra Behn.'

'Who?'

'She was a writer in the seventeenth century. And when he came into my shop, Mr Trigwell asked if I had any copies of her works. It could be just a coincidence that he was waiting close to her tomb.'

'I don't believe in coincidences. I think he chose that place because her tomb was there. Perhaps it was a place he visited regularly?'

'And his killer knew that?'

'Yes.'

Detective Sergeant Joyce was waiting for them outside a tall, red-brick apartment block. It had large sash windows and an elegant portico painted in gleaming white. A uniformed concierge lingered just inside the door.

'Good morning, sir. Mrs Peel.' The young man doffed his hat.

'Morning, Joyce,' said Philip. 'Are you ready?'

'Absolutely.' He rubbed his palms together with enthusiasm.

A stout, grey-haired lady in an apron answered the door of Isabella Trigwell's fourth-floor apartment. 'Golly,' she said as she looked them up and down. 'What an assortment.'

Philip introduced them. 'May we speak with Miss Trigwell?'

'All three of you?'

'Yes please.'

'Well, it can't be for long. Miss Trigwell is tired and extremely distressed, as you can probably imagine. We only buried Mrs Trigwell six weeks ago and now this.'

'I'm aware this is a difficult time for her and we'd like to do all we can to catch the person who did this.'

'Well, in you come then. I'm Mrs Hargreaves, the housekeeper.' She held the door open for them, then led them through a thickly carpeted hallway and into a large, airy room with three large windows set into a bay. The furniture in the room looked expensive: ornately carved, well-polished and upholstered in shades of crimson and gold. Mirrors and paintings of London scenes hung in heavy frames on the walls. Vases and statuettes were displayed on occasional tables and in glass-fronted cabinets. The style of the room was a little old-fashioned and Augusta suspected it was furnished as Isabella Trigwell's mother had wanted it.

Miss Trigwell sat wan faced in a buttoned leather armchair. She looked about thirty and wore a slim-fitting black silk dress. Her pale, long-fingered hands rested in her lap. Her hair was dark and her lips were painted red. The contrast of the lipstick and her pale skin was startling. She was beautiful, even though she looked so pale and fragile. Augusta wasn't sure whether to feel sorry for her or suspect the frailty was an act.

'These gentlemen are from Scotland Yard,' explained Mrs Hargreaves. 'And the lady, Mrs Peel...' she gave Augusta a puzzled glance. 'Are you a detective, too?'

'I'm assisting Detective Inspector Fisher with his investigation,' explained Augusta. 'And I found your brother shortly after he was attacked.'

Miss Trigwell gave a little whimper, as if someone had just given her a sharp prod.

'I realise this is difficult for you, Miss Trigwell,' said Philip as he sat next to Augusta on a velvet red sofa. 'But we need to find out as much about your brother as we possibly can.'

Chapter 15

Miss Trigwell ran her hand across her brow. 'We only buried Mother recently,' she said. Her voice was high and quiet. 'And now Robert! It's too much for one person to cope with.' She picked up a silver case. 'Cigarette?' she asked.

They declined.

Isabella lit her cigarette, then addressed Augusta, 'So you're the lady who found him?'

'Yes. Along with my colleague, Fred Plummer. We tried to do what we could to save him. I'm sorry we couldn't do more.'

'It sounds as though you did all you could.'

Augusta explained how he had visited her bookshop a few days before his death. 'Does the name Symes mean anything to you?' she asked.

'No. Why?'

'When your brother arranged to meet me, he told me his name was Symes.'

'Well, that's a strange thing to do. I have no idea why

he'd do that. He obviously didn't want to admit who he was for some reason.'

'You don't recognise the name Symes?'

'No. And I don't know why he gave you a false name.'

'Were you and your brother close?' Philip asked.

'No. Not really.'

'When did you last see him?'

'A few weeks ago.'

'Can you remember when?'

'The first week of February, I think it was. He came here to help sort through Mother's belongings. He was only here for an hour or two and he didn't do much while he was here, either. I've been doing most of the sorting. Just as I was having to do most of the caring for Mother before she died.'

'How long was she unwell for?'

'About a week. But she was never quite right after Father died. I suppose it must have been some sort of depression and she wasn't an easy person to live with. Robert visited her once a week. I asked for his help, but he refused.'

'What sort of help?'

'Sitting in with her so I could go out, that sort of thing. She didn't like being left alone. She had Annie here.'

'Annie?'

'Mrs Hargreaves. She's been our housekeeper for so long that I call her Annie. But Annie wasn't enough for Mother, she wanted her children with her. Robert should have been here helping me with everything. But I don't suppose he was ever going to do that.'

'What makes you say that?'

'He was too caught up in his own world. I blame the war. He wasn't the only man to come back completely changed from the man he once was. An entire generation damaged. I was sympathetic for a while, but when some-one's that selfish… there's not a great deal you can do.'

'In what way was he selfish?'

'He was only concerned with himself. He adored Mother, and he was very upset when she died. But he took little interest in me. And I suppose it's because I haven't led a particularly interesting life. I could have moved out and made a life for myself, but I never met someone I wished to marry. And Mother was so dependent on me after Father died that I felt I should stay with her. We used to live in Hampstead, but the house felt too big after we lost Father. Mother sold the house, and we bought this flat. That was at the start of the war and Robert went away.' She puffed out a cloud of cigarette smoke.

'How long was he away for?' asked Philip.

'Most of the war. He came back on leave a few times.'

'Which regiment did he serve in?'

'East Surrey. He fought on the Western Front.'

'That must have been a difficult time for him.'

'It must have been, but he didn't talk about it much.'

'Many men these days prefer to forget those times.'

'We all do.'

'Who do you think murdered your brother?' asked Detective Sergeant Joyce.

Philip gave him a sharp glance, as if annoyed by him interrupting the flow of the conversation.

'Who do I think murdered him?' said Miss Trigwell. 'I have no idea!'

'Can you think of anyone who would wish to harm him?' Philip asked. 'Perhaps there was a disagreement with someone?'

'I don't know. I didn't know who his friends and acquaintances were. You'll have to ask them.'

'Did your brother mention anyone was following him?'

'No. Is that what happened?'

'We don't know. Did he ever mention someone called Alfie Smith to you?'

'No. Who's he?'

'Alfred Smith?'

'I don't know who that is.'

'Neither do we, that's why I asked. Robert mentioned his name shortly before he died. Alfred could be the person who murdered your brother or maybe he's the long-lost friend Robert was keen to get in touch with. Do you know if your brother visited Westminster Abbey regularly?'

'I don't know.'

'Did he ever mention Aphra Behn to you?'

'Who?'

'She was a writer.'

'No.'

'Were you aware he enjoyed reading her work?'

'No. We weren't close, as I said.'

'Did you visit Robert in hospital?'

'No, I didn't. I realise that seems cold-hearted of me, but I just assumed he was going to recover. I thought I could visit him at home once he was discharged.'

'Shortly before he died, your brother gave a nurse a number. 78341. Does the number mean anything to you?'

'No. Is it a telephone number?'

'We don't think so. Clearly it meant something to him and we'd like to know what.'

'When did you last see your brother?' asked Detective Sergeant Joyce.

'I've already asked Miss Trigwell that question,' said Philip.

'Oh, did you sir? I apologise.'

'You're asking me a lot of questions,' said Miss Trigwell, stubbing out her cigarette in a crystal ashtray. 'And I'm exhausted. I haven't been sleeping well.'

'I apologise,' said Philip. 'We'll stop the interrogation now. I appreciate your time and I can only hope we'll soon catch the person who did this.' He got to his feet and Augusta and Detective Sergeant Joyce did the same.

Augusta noticed a book about the French Riviera on the table next to Miss Trigwell's chair. 'The south of France,' she said. 'A lovely place.'

'Yes, it is. They have much shorter winters there and the food is wonderful.'

'Sounds perfect,' said Philip. 'Thank you for your time, Miss Trigwell.'

Out on the street, Detective Sergeant Joyce looked up at the apartment building. 'These flats must be worth a few bob.'

'They will be,' said Philip. 'Chelsea is a desirable location. The Hampstead house presumably sold for a good sum and they were able to buy this place with it. There's some expensive furniture in there too.'

'I wonder who inherited the estate after Mrs Trigwell died,' said Augusta.

'Traditionally, the estate goes to the son, doesn't it? But in these modern times, daughters are sometimes considered equally too.'

'It's a question I thought of asking Miss Trigwell just now,' said Augusta. 'But I worried it was a little insensitive after the deaths of her brother and mother within a short space of time.'

'But it's a question we need to know the answer to,' said Philip.

They were interrupted by the roar of a motor car as it

sped along the street then came to a sharp halt close by. It was a blue Sunbeam with large headlamps and a shiny radiator. A man in a boater hat and linen suit jumped out and strode into the apartment building.

'Perhaps Robert inherited the estate after Mrs Trigwell died?' continued Philip.

'Which could have included the apartment Isabella is living in,' said Augusta. 'If Robert inherited it, then he could have chosen to sell it and she would have lost her home.'

'But now that Robert Trigwell has died leaving no descendants, perhaps her home is now her own?'

'His death could have worked out well for her.'

'It's an interesting thought to consider, isn't it?'

'Do you think she's the murderer?' asked Detective Sergeant Joyce.

'It's too early to make a decision about Miss Trigwell,' said Philip. 'But it's important to consider that someone who appears to be a grieving family member could actually be a killer.'

'So we keep an open mind?' asked the young detective.

'Yes, we do. Very good, Joyce. You're learning quickly.'

Chapter 16

'MR ROBSON IS HERE!' called Mrs Hargreaves from the hallway.

Isabella pinched some colour into her cheeks as Douglas swept into the room.

'Are you ready, darling?' He pulled off his boater hat and leant down to kiss her. He was impeccably smart, as usual, and smelt of strong cologne.

'As ready as I'll ever be,' she said.

'Oh no.' He stepped back. 'You're in low-spirits, Issy. What's happened?'

'I've just had a visit from some Scotland Yard detectives and a lady called Mrs Peel who found Robert shortly after he was attacked.'

'That will be the trio of miscreants I saw hanging about outside just now.'

'If only you'd been here earlier, you could have helped me.'

'I'm sorry darling, it wasn't easy making my excuses at work. What did they have to say for themselves?'

'Not a great deal. Mrs Peel told me she did all she

could to save Robert. But she would say that, wouldn't she? Apparently, he visited her bookshop a few days before his death and told her his name was Mr Symes.'

'Symes?'

'Yes. I've no idea what he was up to. And in the hospital he mentioned someone called Alfie Smith to a nurse.'

'Alfie Smith?'

'Yes. Are you just going to repeat everything I say?'

'Sorry darling, I'm just trying to get my head around things. Alfie Symes, perhaps?'

'I don't know. The names mean nothing to me.'

'Nor me.'

'And a number.'

'Which number?'

'A string of them, I can't remember what they were. They meant nothing to me, either. I told the detectives Robert and I weren't close, so I don't know how they expected me to help them.'

Douglas hitched his trousers at the knee and sat on the sofa. 'So Robert visited Mrs Peel in a bookshop, then arranged to meet her in the abbey. She then got there just after he was attacked?'

'Apparently so.'

'What a strange story. Something doesn't seem right about it.'

'Such as what?'

'I don't know. It just sounds off.'

'It does. And Mrs Peel doesn't seem right to me, either. She runs a bookshop and she's also helping Scotland Yard. I've no idea why. She's quite a dowdy lady. Plain-looking clothes.'

'I realise fashion is important to you, Isabella, but you mustn't judge everyone by their appearance.'

His comment irritated her. Why did he have to check her words at a time like this? 'Where have you parked?' she asked.

'Directly outside the door.'

'Good. Then let's go.' She held out her hands, and he helped her up out of the chair. Out in the hallway, she picked up her handbag and put on her black cloche hat. Douglas helped her put on her fur coat and opened the door for her.

'It's a shame I just missed the detectives,' he said, as their footsteps echoed on the stairs. 'You're having a difficult time of it, darling, and you need someone to take care of you. The police can take advantage of people who are feeling hurt and vulnerable. They can trip you up.'

'Trip people up? What do you mean?' The uniformed concierge opened the entrance door for them and they headed for Douglas's blue motor car parked directly in front of the building.

'They can put words in your mouth,' said Douglas, opening the passenger door for her. She slid into the car's luxurious interior and placed her handbag on her knees as Douglas shut the door and went to the front of the car to crank the engine. A moment later, he was sitting next to her in the driver's seat.

'You're saying the police put words in your mouth?' She had to raise her voice over the rumble of the engine.

'With cases like this, they're looking for a suspect, aren't they? The Scotland Yard detectives didn't visit you this morning out of the goodness of their hearts.'

'They asked a lot of questions, but they didn't try to trip me up. The older one was quite handsome, actually.'

'Oh, was he?' The car lurched as he accelerated quickly away. 'Well, don't let him charm you. That's another trick they use.'

'Why are you so determined to persuade me the police are trying to put words in my mouth and trip me up?'

'Because you're a suspect, Isabella.'

'Nonsense!'

'It's not. They have no idea who attacked Robert in the abbey and I think it's unlikely a stranger did it, don't you?'

'Someone who knew him would attack him like that?'

'Yes. Why would a stranger do it?'

'Why would an acquaintance do it?'

'I don't know. Revenge or something like that.'

'For what?'

'We don't know, do we? That's the sort of thing the police will be looking into. What did you ask them?'

'Nothing.'

'Nothing? Aren't you the least bit interested in what theories they might be working on?'

'I can only assume at this stage they don't have any. From what I could tell, they know little about him. And you know yourself he was very private about things. None of us knew much about him, really. The person who knew him best was Mother. He could do no wrong in her eyes.'

She felt the familiar wave of envy wash over her as she said these words. She distracted herself by looking out of the window at the shoppers on King's Road.

Chapter 17

HALF AN HOUR LATER, Isabella and Douglas sat in the Belgravia offices of the law firm Barrington, Harris and Wilson. Mr Barrington had been the Trigwell family solicitor for more years than she could remember. The plump, grey-haired man sat at his vast mahogany desk with an appropriately sombre expression on his face.

'I take it that no will has been found in Mr Trigwell's home?' he said.

'No. I've looked high and low for it,' said Isabella. 'It's not been easy with the police rummaging around in there too, they've made quite a mess. But there's no sign of a will.'

'It's as I feared then. I've informed you previously that we had no record of Mr Trigwell making a will with us. Did he mention to you he'd written a will?'

'No. He never mentioned it at all.'

'It appears, then, that he died intestate.'

'So what happens to his estate?' asked Douglas.

'In these cases, it passes to the closest relative.'

'So that's Isabella?'

'Yes, Miss Trigwell would be considered the closest relative, as her brother never married and he had no issue. There's still a possibility that he made a will and it hasn't been found yet.'

'I think that's unlikely,' said Douglas. 'You've gone through all his papers, haven't you, Isabella?'

'Yes.'

She felt the corners of her mouth trying to lift. Could it be possible the entire family estate was now hers? After years of assuming everything would go to her younger brother, she now found herself in a new position. A lady of property.

She assumed a mournful expression, keen to show she was unmoved by this development.

'What's the value of the estate?' asked Douglas.

'I can't tell you that at present,' said Mr Barrington. 'The estate was obviously valued after Mrs Trigwell's recent passing, however, we need to include Mr Trigwell's assets as well. That could take a little while because he doesn't appear to have kept many records.'

'Surely you have an idea of how much is in his bank account?'

'May I ask, Mr Robson, if you're a relative?'

'No, I'm not a relative. Just a friend of Miss Trigwell's.'

'In which case, I need to make it clear that I will primarily deal with Miss Trigwell. As you're not considered a beneficiary, I'm sure you'll appreciate that I'm unable to answer your questions directly.'

'Of course.' He held up his palms in a gesture of acceptance. 'I'm merely here to support Miss Trigwell.'

'That's very thoughtful of you, Mr Robson.'

. . .

'Well, what do you make of that then, darling?' said Douglas. 'Looks like you're rich!' He gave a wide grin as he held open the passenger door of the motor car for Isabella.

'I suppose it's only natural everything should go to me. I'm the only surviving member of my family.'

Douglas cranked the car, then climbed into the seat beside her. 'You are indeed. It's just as well Robert didn't have a wife and children, isn't it? Otherwise, they'd have inherited it all instead. It's worked out quite well.'

'I wouldn't describe it as that. I'd much rather my mother and brother were still here.'

'Even though the pair of them annoyed you?'

'Yes! Do you think, for one moment, that I'm happy they're dead?' She let out a cry, pulled out her handkerchief, and buried her face in it.

'No, of course not. I apologise, Isabella, my words sounded far more thoughtless than I'd intended them to be.'

He steered the car through traffic in Eaton Square and Isabella made a point of sobbing loudly.

'Oh come now.' He patted her knee. 'Don't cry like this while I'm driving, darling. I can't comfort you!'

As they approached Sloane Square, the traffic stopped. Isabella dried her eyes and Douglas tapped on the steering wheel impatiently. 'What's going on?' He wound down his window and craned his head out. 'What chaos! Is there no officer directing the traffic?'

'Don't be so impatient, dear,' said Isabella. 'There's no hurry.'

'There is. I have to be home well before dinner.'

'Why?'

'Diana's sister and her husband are visiting us.'

She felt a bitter taste of resentment. 'Do you have to see them?'

'Yes, of course. I can't miss a visit from my in-laws and Diana's expecting me.'

'Just tell her a lie.'

'I've already told her lots of lies, Issy. She's quite suspicious now.'

'But you have to tell her the truth soon.'

'And I will. Just not today.'

'But you told me you're estranged from her!'

'I am. But I still have some duties.'

'So you're just leaving me to go back to your wife?'

'I'm afraid I have to today.'

Isabella broke out into more sobs, which she knew he would hate.

'Oh come now, darling. I can visit you again tomorrow.'

'Tomorrow isn't today though, is it? I need you today!'

'I realise that, but some things just can't be helped.'

Isabella continued to cry, hoping he'd give in to her before they got back to her flat.

Chapter 18

'What a happy budgerigar!' said the Irish lady in blue and fox fur. 'He's singing away there in his little birdcage.'

'He's actually a canary,' said Augusta, putting *The Tenant of Wildfell Hall* into a striped paper bag.

'Oh, he's a canary, is he? I apologise. I hope I haven't offended him.'

Augusta smiled and handed her the bag. 'He's often mistaken for a budgie, so he doesn't mind.'

'That's lucky then, he's a very tolerant little fellow.' The lady's piercing eyes sparkled with humour. She had become a regular customer since Augusta had recommended *Wuthering Heights* and had now purchased four books by the Brontë sisters.

'I hope you enjoy the book.'

'I'm sure I will, thank you.'

As she left the shop, a man in a dark suit strode in. He headed straight for the staircase and climbed the stairs. Augusta eyed him, noticing that he didn't seem interested in the bookshelves.

After a minute or so, there was no further sign of the

man, so Augusta decided to investigate. She climbed the stairs to the mezzanine floor and saw it was empty of customers.

'He's vanished!' she exclaimed. She tried the handle of the door in the corner. It was locked.

She stormed back down the stairs and marched into the workshop where Fred was making a pot of tea. 'I've just seen a man using our shop as a shortcut!' she said. 'The cheek of it!'

'Did you see him go through the secret door?'

'No. But I saw him go up the stairs. And when I followed him, he'd vanished! He could only have gone through the door.'

'He must have done.'

'I'm going to speak to them about it,' said Augusta.

Her heart thudded as she walked out of her shop and jabbed her finger into the doorbell at the next door. A new sign had appeared above it: "Fitzwilliam and Harper Bookkeeping Services".

After a short wait, the door was answered by a young, pale-haired man with a red complexion.

'I'm Mrs Peel,' said Augusta. 'I own the bookshop beneath your premises. I would like to request that you and your colleagues refrain from using the door inside my shop to access your offices.'

'I'm sorry?' The young man's mouth hung open.

Augusta took in a patient breath and tried another explanation. 'Someone in your office is using my shop as a shortcut. I would like to request that he stops doing it, please.'

'A shortcut?'

'Yes. He walks through my shop to get to and from his office. There's no need for him to do that because there's a perfectly good entrance here where we're both standing.'

The gormless young man glanced about him as if he'd only just noticed the doorway.

'So do you think you could pass my message onto your colleagues?'

He nodded in reply, but Augusta had little confidence the message would be relayed as she had asked.

Back in her bookshop, Fred stood by the telephone. 'I've just spoken to Philip,' he said. 'He told me he's made good progress and asked if you could visit him at Scotland Yard.'

'When?'

'Now.'

'Now? Did he say what progress had been made?'

'No. But if you're happy to go, Mrs Peel, then I can look after everything here.'

'Thank you, Fred. And if you catch one of those book-keepers walking through here again, you have my permission to box his ears.'

'Augusta!' She couldn't resist smiling when Philip greeted her in his office. It was good to see him happy. 'Thank you for making the journey. I have a very specific reason for inviting you here.'

'Is that so?'

He pointed to a large paper bag on his desk which was printed with the word "Evidence". 'I thought you might like to see the weapon.'

Augusta shuddered. 'Alright then.'

Philip pulled out a desk drawer and put on a pair of gloves. Then he pulled a folded cloth out of the paper bag, lay it on the desk and unfolded it to reveal a knife.

'It's been cleaned and examined,' said Philip. 'We've found some fingerprints on the handle, but they appear to belong to more than one person.'

'That complicates matters.'

'It does.'

'It looks like an ordinary kitchen knife.'

'That's because it is. The blade is five inches long, and the manufacturer is Jackson's of Sheffield. It's a moderately priced kitchen knife which can be bought in any reputable ironmongers in London.'

'So it's going to be difficult to trace the killer from the knife.'

'Yes, unless we can identify the fingerprints. I visited Westminster Abbey this morning and spoke to the dean. He told me that none of the clergymen or visitors appear to have seen anything suspicious around the time of Robert Trigwell's attack. I think the location the knife was found gives us a clue. It was dark enough for the killer to hide on the square of grass with no one noticing them. Perhaps they waited for Mr Trigwell there and then returned to the hiding spot before skulking off when the coast was clear.'

'So the attacker could have been hiding there when Fred and I found Robert injured?' Augusta shuddered. 'What a thought.'

'It is, isn't it? The dean and his team recall seeing Robert Trigwell in the abbey on previous occasions and they knew he liked to sit in the cloisters. I think the murderer knew it was something he did regularly. I think they must have lain in wait for him there.'

'That makes sense.'

'After my visit to the abbey, I met Sergeant Wilcox at Mr Trigwell's flat and he showed me what they've found there. A chatty neighbour, Mrs Evans, talked at us for a while. She liked Mr Trigwell but knew little about his personal affairs. We've come across a few personal papers which will be passed to the family now. They don't give us many clues, unfortunately.'

'There must be something in them.'

Philip opened his notebook. 'I made a note of what's been found. Birth certificate. That didn't really tell us anything new. He was born in Hampstead in 1894. He went to school in the area and joined the army when he was twenty years old. No mention of the name Symes on anything, so I don't know why he mentioned that name to you. His British War Medal and Allied Victory Medal were found in an envelope. The British War Medal states he was a private in the East Surrey Regiment, service number 39872.'

An idea struck Augusta so suddenly it felt like an electric shock. 'That could be it!'

'I'm sorry?'

'The number we've been trying to identify. Perhaps it's a regimental number?'

'What is it again?' He flipped back through his notebook. '78341?'

'Yes.'

'I suppose it could be, couldn't it? Alfie Smith's service number? What a thought. Well, there's only one way to find out, and that's to check the War Office records.'

Chapter 19

THE WAR OFFICE was on Whitehall, a short walk from Scotland Yard. It was an imposing building of grey stone with a columned facade and two ornate turrets. Inside, a grand staircase dominated the entrance hall. It divided into two before climbing to an upper gallery with an elegant balustrade. An enormous chandelier hung from the high ceiling and large portraits decorated the walls.

Philip made some enquiries at the desk and they were joined moments later by a records officer called Mr Gower. He was a broad man who walked with a limp and the first thing he noticed was Philip's walking stick.

'Ah ha!' he said. 'A fellow injured former serviceman?'

'Intelligence.'

'Intelligence?' His eyes widened. 'How fascinating! Your records are probably stored here too, although I won't be allowed to look at them. Top secret! Only the top brass can look at them. In fact, you wouldn't be able to look at them yourself. Isn't that an amusing thought?'

'It certainly is. And I'm sure you could say the same for Mrs Peel here. She worked with me.'

'You were both intelligence officers? I feel humbled by your company indeed.'

'There's no need.'

'Alright then. Perhaps you can tell me how I can help you?'

'We have a number which we believe is an Army service number. We'd like to find out if there are some related records we can look at.'

'I see. Do you have the name of the gentleman?'

'We think it might be Alfie Smith.'

'You *think*?'

'Yes. It's possible we're mistaken.'

'Smith is a horribly common surname. No records officer enjoys looking for someone with the name Smith. Regiment?'

'We could make a guess at that. The gentleman who passed on the number served in the East Surrey Regiment.'

'Well, that's a start, I suppose. Let's go and have a look at the records, shall we? Follow me. I don't walk particularly fast, I'm afraid.'

Augusta walked with the two limping gentlemen along a corridor which grew less grand the further they walked from the main entrance.

'I'm afraid the records aren't kept in the pretty part of the building,' said Mr Gower. 'They're in the basement. What I affectionately call the bowels of the building.'

'Nice.'

He pushed open a door with opaque safety glass and it opened into a stairwell which was cold and musty. There was dim lighting on the walls and the steps were concrete.

'I would lead the way,' said Mr Gower. 'But my progress down these steps is usually slow. I can imagine it's much the same for you, Detective Inspector Fisher.'

'It is indeed.'

'Perhaps you'd like to go on ahead, Mrs Peel?' said the records officer. 'You'll find a set of double doors at the bottom. Just go on through and we'll see you there.'

Augusta felt it would be more polite to keep pace with them, but Mr Gower presumably felt uncomfortable having someone watch him slowly descend the steps. She went on ahead of them and reached the double doors as he had described. They were both glazed with the same opaque safety glass as the door which had opened onto the stairwell.

The door she pulled open was heavy, and she closed it slowly behind her, aware it would be a minute or two before the men arrived.

The ceiling was low and iron pendant lamps hung from it, emitting a dim and flickering glow. There was a thin army green carpet beneath her feet and rows of metal shelving stretched as far as she could see. Each row had a number, and each shelf was crammed with paper files. Each file was tagged with a number. Augusta walked along a row, astonished by the volume of paperwork. She turned the corner at the end of the row and tried to comprehend the number of rows stretching away from her on either side. The air felt close and had an acid, papery smell.

She heard the door open. Philip and Mr Gower had arrived. She made her way back to the door to meet them.

'There you are, Mrs Peel,' said Mr Gower. 'You've not got lost yet, then?'

'I didn't stray too far for fear of that happening.'

Mr Gower chuckled and limped off to the far end of the basement. Augusta and Philip followed. They reached a desk which had shelves of leather-bound volumes behind it. Mr Gower manoeuvred himself into the space between the leather volumes and the desk.

'Shall we begin with the East Surrey Regiment?' he asked.

'It seems a good place to start,' said Philip.

'Take a seat,' Mr Gower gestured at two wooden chairs before searching through the leather volumes. 'Let's begin with this one.' He pulled out a hefty volume and placed it on the desk.

'Now this handy little book will tell us where to locate the records on the shelves you see around you.'

'Excellent,' said Philip. 'We're looking for someone called Robert Trigwell.'

'Not Alfie Smith?'

'We have more details for Mr Trigwell. And we hope that, by finding him, we will also find Alfie Smith. We're making the assumption the two men served together.'

'I see. Now this Trigwell chap, was he a member of the New Army?' This was a reference to the men who were enrolled in the army after the outbreak of war.

'I suppose so,' said Philip. 'Let's assume he was a civilian before the war.'

'That helps us,' said Mr Gower. 'It means we can narrow our search to the seventh to fourteenth battalions of the East Surrey Regiment.'

'Narrow?'

'Seven battalions isn't very narrow, is it? Not with a little over a thousand men in each.'

'I shall state the obvious,' said Philip. 'But that's over seven thousand men in total.'

'Indeed. And we're only making an assumption he joined the New Army. If he didn't, then he may have been in divisions one to six.'

'We could be here all week!'

'We could. Do you have any idea which battalion this gentleman served in?'

Philip leafed through his notebook. 'I don't think I wrote that down. How silly of me! Do you have a telephone I could use? I need to telephone the Yard and find out that information.'

'Of course. It's on the wall by the door to the stairs. To make it easier for us, we need the battalion, then the letter of the company. As you know, each battalion has four companies. Then the number of the platoon would serve us well, too. That would narrow it down to about fifty men. Any information on the section would help as well.'

Philip went off to make the telephone call and Augusta hoped Alfie Smith had served in the same platoon as Robert Trigwell. Otherwise, they were in for a long search.

'Difficult to believe we're beneath the streets of White-hall here, isn't it?' Mr Gower said to Augusta. 'All those people walking above our heads with no clue we're down here!'

'Do you get many visitors?'

'Yes, a few. But they don't like to come here unless they really have to. Although I must say the Secretary of State for War visited a few weeks ago. That took us by surprise. Mr Winston Churchill. Nice of him to take an interest in us.'

'I know his name. Was he looking for something in particular?'

'No, he just wanted to have a look around and see what we do here. Pleasant chap. He served in Asquith's government before the war and commanded the 6th Royal Scots Fusiliers for a time during the war. We're not normally visited by the important people. Usually, we're just shuffling around down here like forgotten little moles.'

Philip returned, and his expression suggested he had successfully discovered some new information. 'The eighth battalion,' he said, 'number seven platoon in B Company.

Those are the details for Robert Trigwell. I hope we can find Alfie Smith's name and service number in the records too.'

Mr Gower turned the pages, then ran his finger down a list. 'Yes, we can retrieve those records. Any idea of the section?'

'I'm afraid not.'

'Never mind. Let's fetch the files and have a look through them.'

After retrieving the records from the shelves, the three of them began searching the lists of names. Philip was the first to find Robert Trigwell. 'Here he is!' he said proudly. 'Although we knew we'd find him here. A Private in the Rifle Section.'

'Is there an Alfie in the same section?' asked Augusta, getting up and peering over his shoulder.

'Yes!' Philip pointed him out. 'Alfred Smith. Does his service number match the one Mr Trigwell gave out?'

Augusta read out the number. '78341'

'That's it!' said Philip.

'Wonderful!' said Mr Gower. 'It looks like you've found your man. It proved not to be quite so tricky after all.'

'Robert Trigwell's long-lost friend was Alfred Smith, and they served together in the war,' said Philip.

'What about Symes?' said Augusta.

'The name Robert Trigwell mentioned to you? Let's have a look.'

After some searching, they couldn't find any record of someone with the name Symes.

'Well at least we found Mr Smith,' said Philip. 'The next question is, where is he now?'

Chapter 20

THE FOLLOWING day was sunny but cold. Birds wheeled in the air above the boats on the Thames. Alfred caught his hat just before it blew away, then spotted a familiar figure walking towards him.

'Sylvia?'

'Surprise!' She grinned. 'You often tell me how you like to walk along the riverside during your lunch breaks, Alfred, so I thought I'd come and find you here!'

'Well that's a lovely surprise indeed.' He leaned forward and kissed her cheek. She wore a woollen hat and a thick coat.

'It's difficult seeing each other now that you won't visit us anymore,' she said.

'I will visit again, I promise. It's just going to be difficult with your father.'

'He spends most of his time in his study, he'll barely notice you!' She leant against the wall and surveyed the river. 'It's some view from here, isn't it? The Houses of Parliament really are quite beautiful and I could watch the boats here for hours. There's always something going on, isn't there?'

Alfred felt encouraged by Sylvia's surprise visit. Despite her father's disapproval, she was still keen to see him. His only worry was that she seemed quite confident Mr Golding would eventually accept him. He couldn't imagine that happening.

'So tell me, Sylvia. Are you sure you want to proceed with our engagement? Even if your father disapproves?'

She turned to him with a smile. Her cheeks were red from the cold breeze. 'Yes Alfred! We love each other, don't we?'

'Yes, we do.'

'Then what else do we need?'

He was about to reply when he noticed someone approach. He turned to see his friend and fellow student Ernest Morrison. 'Smith?' he said cautiously. 'I'm sorry to interrupt, but there are two people here to see you.'

'Who?'

Morrison made way for a man with a walking stick and a woman with wavy auburn hair. They both wore dark overcoats and hats.

'Mr Alfred Smith?' asked the gentleman.

'Yes. That's me.'

'Detective Inspector Fisher of Scotland Yard.' Alfred felt his heart thud as the detective reached into his pocket and showed him his warrant card. 'And this is my colleague, Mrs Peel. May we have a word?'

Chapter 21

ALFRED SMITH WAS A TALL, thin man with handsome features and fair hair. His expression was rigid, and Augusta suspected he felt unnerved by their appearance.

'May I ask what it's regarding?'

'Mr Robert Trigwell. Did you know him?'

Alfred paled. 'Erm. Yes, I did.'

'Who is he?' asked the young woman at his side.

'Someone I knew in the war.' He turned back to Philip and Augusta. 'This is Miss Golding, my fiancée. Of sorts.'

'*Of sorts*?' said Miss Golding.

'Well, we're just finalising it, aren't we, Sylvia? In fact, we were discussing it just before we were interrupted.'

'We apologise for the interruption,' said Philip. 'But we need to speak to you as a matter of urgency.'

'Who's Robert Trigwell?' asked Sylvia.

'He died last week after an attack in Westminster Abbey.'

'*Him?*' Her eyes widened. She turned back to Mr Smith. 'You knew him?'

'Yes. A long time ago.'

'But you didn't tell me!'

'I read about it in the paper the other day and I wasn't sure if it was the same fellow I knew.'

'But you didn't choose to mention it at all? I would have thought that even if you suspected you knew him, then you would have said. Everyone has been talking about the murder, it's dreadful!'

'It certainly is,' said Philip. 'And we need to ask you a few questions, Mr Smith.'

'Can't it wait until later?'

'I'm afraid not.'

Alfred sighed. 'I'm sorry, Sylvia, but I need to speak to the detectives in private.'

'You want me to leave?'

'I don't *want* you to leave, but I think it's probably for the best while I speak to the police.'

'Very well.' Her lips tightened. 'And when you've finished work for the day, perhaps you'll have the courtesy to call on me and explain what's going on!'

She strode off along the riverside, her heels clicking on the ground.

'I'm sorry,' said Philip. 'We appear to have dropped you in it.'

Alfred rubbed his brow. 'I'll explain it to her later.'

'Is there a lot to explain?'

'No.' He met Philip's eye. 'Not much at all. How did you find me?'

'A bit of research in the War Office records and then the Electoral Roll. Is there somewhere quiet we can talk?'

'We can probably find a room in the medical school. Follow me.'

. . .

A short while later, they sat in a pleasant study overlooking the river. Westminster lay on the opposite bank. If Alfred Smith was the long-lost friend Robert Trigwell had been searching for, then he hadn't been far away. And in a twist of fate, he was a medical student at the same hospital Robert had died in.

'So you didn't mention Robert Trigwell to Miss Golding?' Philip said. 'Why was that?'

'I've already explained, I read about the incident in the newspaper but I wasn't completely sure he was the Robert I knew.'

'Very well. I'll remind you, however, that I'm a detective inspector investigating a murder, so if I suspect you're hiding something—'

'I've nothing to hide!' His response startled Augusta. He seemed to realise this and checked himself. 'I'm sorry. It's been a tricky few weeks. I asked Sylvia's father for her hand in marriage and he refused to give us our blessing. He dislikes me.'

'I'm sorry to hear it.'

'Sylvia thinks we should get married regardless, but I don't think she realises what it will be like having parents who disapprove of her husband.'

'That can't be easy. I'm sorry we called on you at a difficult time, Mr Smith. We want to speak to you because it seems Robert Trigwell was keen to find you.'

'Was he?' He pulled at his collar and Augusta wondered why he was so nervous.

'So much so that he actually visited Mrs Peel and asked her to find a long-lost friend.'

His eyebrows raised. 'Goodness. You have expertise in such things, Mrs Peel?'

'Not really,' she replied. 'I'm not sure why he thought I could help.'

'Mrs Peel is playing down her abilities,' said Philip. 'She's an excellent investigator.'

'What did he say about me?'

'Very little. That was the trouble.' Philip went on to explain how Robert Trigwell had arranged to meet Augusta, been found seriously injured and then passed on Mr Smith's details to the nurse.

'He remembered my service number?' He gave a laugh. 'I can't even remember it myself. In fact, I deliberately forgot it.'

'We understand you served alongside Mr Trigwell.'

'Yes. We were in the same section. Our battalion was sent to France in the summer of 1915. We were part of the infamous football attack the following year.'

'I remember reading about that,' said Augusta. 'You were there?'

'Football attack?' said Philip.

'Surely you remember it being reported?' said Augusta. 'I don't think I do.'

'The first of July 1916,' said Mr Smith. 'The first day of the Somme offensive. We were at Carnoy. During the previous week, we had bombarded the German lines with artillery and the generals said their defences had been wiped out. We suspected differently as the enemy had been shelling our trenches in retaliation. But despite that, the decision was made to advance. At half-past seven that morning, Captain Nevill and Lieutenant Soames led the first advance. They headed out into the smoke, the pair of them kicking footballs! Such bravery in the jaws of death. They did it to distract us and put our minds at ease and I'd say it worked.' He paused. 'They were brave men. Both were killed that day. Nearly half our battalion lost their lives or were wounded on that one day alone.'

Silence followed.

Augusta had read about the horrors of the Western Front. She knew almost twenty thousand British soldiers had died on that one day, the first of July 1916.

'Many better men than me should still be here,' said Alfred Smith. 'I don't think I'll ever reconcile myself with that.'

Philip nodded, and the silence continued.

'We left Carnoy about three weeks later,' said Mr Smith eventually. 'And went on to Bois Grenier, then Thiepval… I won't bore you with the rest. Somehow Symes and I got through it.'

'Symes?'

'Sorry, I meant Trigwell. Symes was a name I had for him. It was the name of an old schoolfriend whom he reminded me of.'

'When did you last see him?' asked Philip.

'At the end of the war. How long ago was that? Two and a half years, I suppose.'

'Did you communicate with each other after that?'

'No.' He scratched at his neck, leaving a red mark.

'You didn't exchange letters? Christmas cards?'

'No.'

'So you were friends during the war, but didn't have any contact after that?'

'That's right. And I don't think that's unusual. Once we returned, we were all keen to put the horrors behind us and get on with our lives on civvy street. I'm afraid I became quite selfish in that respect. I didn't wish to reminisce about those days with anyone. All I wanted to do was find decent employment and marry.'

'You wanted to forget about the war?' asked Philip.

'Yes. Who doesn't?'

'And you wanted to forget about Robert Trigwell?'

'I didn't say that.'

'But you denied knowing him to Miss Golding?'

'I didn't deny it. I just chose not to mention it.'

'So can we ask you to be truthful now?' asked Augusta. 'Did you know who Robert Trigwell was when you read about his death?'

He paused and wiped his brow again. 'Yes,' he said. 'I knew who he was. And I don't understand why anyone would want to harm him like that.'

Chapter 22

'I FIND it quite remarkable that no one seems able to tell us much about Robert Trigwell,' said Philip as they crossed Westminster Bridge back towards New Scotland Yard. 'Either no one knew him very well or they're lying to us.'

'I suspect it's the latter,' said Augusta.

'I suspect so, too. But it's so frustrating!'

'You need patience,' said Augusta. 'Isn't that what you're teaching Detective Sergeant Joyce?'

'Yes. But who bothers to follow their own advice? And besides, I can be patient when I really need to be. Do you remember how we waited in that Belgian forest for three days?'

'Watching the railway line just outside Roeseloare? How can I forget?' Augusta laughed.

She and Philip had been tasked with notifying the British when an ordnance train had arrived at Roeseloare to supply the German front line with weapons and ammunition. 'Intelligence told us the train would be there on the first day,' she said, 'and it didn't turn up until two days later! We had to work shifts, taking turns to stay awake and watch for it. I remember feeling quite fed up by day three.'

'And then we both accidentally fell asleep at the same time. Do you remember? We panicked for a while, thinking we'd missed it.'

'You fell asleep on your shift.'

'No Augusta, you fell asleep on your shift!'

They both laughed. 'I remember how we argued about it at the time,' she said. 'And then the train eventually turned up and there was no need to bicker about it anymore.'

'I was overjoyed when it finally turned up. What a good feeling that was, I'll never forget it. It was quite a fire-work display, wasn't it?' said Philip.

'Awful when you think about it.'

She could clearly recall the explosions and the wall of flame which had engulfed the depot. She would never forget the screams of men. She paused and looked out over the river. She couldn't think about the attack for too long.

'It had to be done,' said Philip, stopping beside her. 'The destruction of that train meant the German soldiers had fewer shells and bullets to fire at men like Trigwell and Smith. War is brutal. None of us had any choice in the matter at the time.'

'You're right. And waiting in that forest was better than being a cafe girl.'

Augusta had spent some more months in Roeseloare pretending to be a Belgian waitress. She had waited on the German soldiers in the hope of overhearing their conver-sations.

'You were a good cafe girl,' said Philip.

'Thank you. But I never stopped feeling nervous. Whenever I had to converse with those men, I was worried they would realise who I really was.'

'But they didn't.'

'I think one or two suspected me. And that's when I asked to be moved to another cafe.'

'It was certainly thrilling.'

'That's one way of describing it.'

'But it was!'

They leant on the bridge wall and watched a coal barge pass beneath. Plumes of steam rose from its funnel.

'I realise this may be a strange thing to say,' said Philip, 'but when you're living life like that - not knowing if you're about to get caught or die horribly - it brings life into sharper focus. Don't you think? There's no worrying about the past or the future. All your effort goes into survival. You take each day at a time and complete your tasks to your best ability. And at the end of each day, you offer up a grateful prayer that you weren't caught. It was a horrible, yet simple, life.'

'It wasn't life. It was survival.'

'True.'

She turned to him. 'You're speaking as if you preferred those times to now.'

'No, I don't think anyone can say they preferred those dreadful days when we were at war. That would be ridiculous, wouldn't it? But the difference these days is that we have time for rumination. And a little too much reflection on what's gone wrong.'

'Your marriage, you mean?'

Philip met her gaze. 'Yes, I suppose I'm referring to that. Thinking about it becomes repetitive after a while. And I never feel any better for it. During the war, we were kept busy for every minute, every hour. There was no time to dwell on things. I think that's what I miss.'

'You don't like time to think?'

'Not at the moment, no. Anyway,' he checked his watch, 'let's get on with things. We need to find more people who knew Robert Trigwell. I think we should attend the funeral and see who turns up. What do you say?'

'That's a good idea.'

Chapter 23

'Miss Trigwell, on behalf of J Baker's management and staff, I offer you our most sincere condolences.'

'Oh, thank you so much.' She held out her hand and he shook it. Her features were half-concealed behind her black lace veil, but he could see she was a beautiful young woman. 'You're attending the funeral as a representative of Robert's employer?' she asked.

'Yes, my name is Simon Granger and your brother worked for me. He was a hard-working and diligent young man.' Robert had been a little too diligent for his own good, but Simon chose not to dwell on that now. 'I'm very sorry for your tragic loss.'

'Thank you. It means so much to me that you came.'

Few people had attended Robert Trigwell's funeral. They had barely filled a pew in the chapel at Brompton Cemetery.

A man in a black suit stood next to Miss Trigwell. He held out his hand. 'I'm Mr Robson. Thank you for coming, Mr Granger.'

'It's my pleasure.' They fixed each other's gaze, both pretending they had never met before.

A stout, grey-haired lady was also present, she was with Miss Trigwell and Mr Robson. Also present was a tall, thin young man with fair hair and a lady wearing an old-fashioned, broad-brimmed black hat.

They watched glumly as the coffin was placed into the hearse. Then they followed the hearse as it made its way along the broad path through the cemetery. There had been a frost overnight, and the headstones and tombs were covered in a light dusting of ice. Icy, white spider webs were strung between them.

The lady in the old-fashioned hat fell into step beside him. 'Terrible shame,' she muttered. 'Such an awful tragedy, isn't it? He was such a pleasant young man. I was his neighbour. Mrs Evans is the name.'

'Mr Granger.'

'Nice to meet you. Robert lived in the flat across the corridor from me. The first thing I knew about it was when the police came knocking at my door. They wanted to know if I'd heard or seen anything suspicious. It was the morning after and I can't tell you how shocked I was. I knew Robert enjoyed visiting the abbey because it was so peaceful there. London's so busy and noisy, isn't it? There aren't many places you can go to get away from it all. The parks are nice but even they get busy too, especially on a sunny day. Robert wasn't a God-fearing man, but I think he liked the sanctuary of the abbey.'

Talkative people irritated Simon. He clenched his teeth as she continued.

'He was the peaceful, quiet type. He liked his books and his solitude. You wouldn't believe the palaver that's been going on at his flat this past week. The police have been in and out and asking all sorts of questions. They want to know who he's been seen with, has anyone unsavoury been hanging around and looking suspicious, that sort of thing. I haven't seen anyone, and he rarely had visitors. He hadn't lived there long, about two years in all. He kept himself to himself, but he was very polite whenever I spoke to him. I felt very happy with him as a neighbour and now I'm nervous about who's going to move in there next. He told me his mother died, and he was very upset about that, I could tell. He adored her. I never saw her visit him, though, and I never saw his sister either. That's her over there, isn't it?'

'Yes.'

'And her husband, I suppose.'

'He's not her husband.'

'He's not? How intriguing! What's his name then?'

'Douglas Robson, I believe.'

'I don't remember Robert mentioning him. He didn't tell me much about his sister other than she was living with his mother. He told me his mother had been in low spirits ever since the death of his father. A lot of tragedy in the family by the sound of things. And I don't know the sister at all, but I imagine she must be having an awful time. First losing her mother and now losing her brother. And in such awful circumstances! A sudden death is one thing, but murder? It's absolutely terrible, I don't know how you get over such things. Her man friend seems fond of her, doesn't he? I suppose he must be a lot of support to her at a time like this. And she's a rich lady, have you heard? Her mother left a good fortune when she died and that passed to Robert. But now, with him gone, everything goes to her. Not that the money is any comfort to her at a time like this but in the coming years she'll be grateful for it, I'm sure.'

She paused and glanced around. 'It's awfully sad there isn't a bigger turnout. Robert wasn't the sort to have lots of friends. Not everyone does, do they? Some like to keep to themselves and there's nothing wrong with that whatsoever. I wonder who the young gentleman is? He told me his name was James Godwin, but I don't remember Robert mentioning him. Apparently, they served together in the war, but they hadn't seen each other since then. How did you know Robert?'

'We were work colleagues.'

'At J Baker's? That's nice. He loved his job, did Robert.'

'Did he?'

'Yes, he spoke proudly of his work there. I must say I do like your teashops, they're so much better than those Lyons Corner Houses. I expect Robert's colleagues were upset, weren't they?'

'They were shocked.'

'I can imagine!'

'No one could understand how someone so mild-mannered could have suffered such a violent end.'

'That's exactly what I think! How could someone have done such a thing? Just dreadful. I hope the police catch them soon.'

The hearse came to a slow stop, and the coffin was carried to a grave beside a freshly dug mound of earth.

'The committal is always the worst bit,' whispered Mrs Evans. 'Do you find that too? It's just so… final. Who are those people over there?'

Simon noticed a man and a woman in black coats standing a short distance away. The man leant on a walking stick.

'Oh, I recognise him now,' said Mrs Evans. 'He spoke to me just the other day. He's a Scotland Yard detective.'

'Really?' Simon's stomach gave a lurch.

'Perhaps he's here to see who's turned up. I don't know who the woman is, though. Maybe his wife?'

Chapter 24

'So who have we got at the graveside?' Philip whispered to Augusta as they watched the committal for Robert Trigwell. 'Isabella Trigwell, Annie Hargreaves the housekeeper and Alfred Smith. It's interesting to see him here, isn't it? I recognise that other woman as Robert's neighbour, Mrs Evans. Now who's that man standing next to Miss Trigwell?'

'I recognise him,' said Augusta. 'He pulled up in his car just after we left her flat.'

'Now that's interesting. Perhaps he's courting her? I don't recognise that gentleman there with the square face and wide shoulders. I wonder who he is?'

'Let's find out once it's over.'

The vicar's voice carried across the headstones, but he was too far away for the words to be distinct.

'I'm afraid to say I dashed off before Joyce could join me this morning,' whispered Philip. 'I feel a bit guilty about it now. It's not his fault his father is the commissioner.'

'He could have chosen a different career.'

'I suppose he could have done.'

'So it is his fault because he's chosen an easy path. He should have to work his way up the ranks like everyone else.'

'Agreed. Although I can't say I did that.'

'You proved yourself with your work during the war. That's why you were awarded with the position.'

'I suppose you could see it like that. And I suppose I wouldn't mind Joyce too much if he was good at his job. But the trouble is, he's rather clueless. Oh look. Have they finished now?' The group by the graveside was beginning to disperse. 'Let's grab that square-faced chap.'

The square-faced man's dour expression suggested he didn't want to talk to the police. He told them his name was Simon Granger, and he was representing the company which Robert had worked for. His hands were thrust deep into the pockets of his overcoat and he was stamping his feet as if he were cold and impatient to get away.

'When was the last time you saw Mr Trigwell?' asked Philip.

'At work. On the day of his death.'

'And how did he seem?'

'His usual self.'

'He didn't appear to be bothered by anything?'

'No. But if he had been, he wasn't the sort of man to show it.'

'Did he mention whether anyone was upset with him?'

'No.'

'Did he say if anyone had been following him?'

'No. And that doesn't mean they weren't, he just wouldn't have said. He was a quiet man. He kept himself to himself. Mrs Evans knows much more about him than me.' He pointed at a lady in a large black hat.

'Yes, I've already spoken to her,' said Philip. 'How did you get on with Mr Trigwell?'

'Fine. We were acquaintances. We weren't friendly.'

'How long did you work with him for?'

'About a year.'

'And on the day of his death, did he mention to you he was going to Westminster Abbey?'

'No. It wouldn't be the sort of thing he would have mentioned.'

'Do you know if he mentioned his intention to any other colleagues?'

'No, I don't know. He may have done. But I knew nothing about it. Mrs Evans told me he liked to go to the abbey and it was the first I'd heard of it. I'm sorry I'm not much help, Detective Inspector.'

He stepped away as if keen to move on.

'Very well, thank you for speaking to me Mr Granger.'

They watched him walk briskly off down the cemetery path. 'He was keen to get away, wasn't he?' said Augusta.

'He was.'

'If a colleague of mine was murdered and a Scotland Yard detective asked me questions about it, I would like to be as helpful as possible,' said Augusta. 'Perhaps that's just the way I am. I think if someone seems hurried, defensive and keen to distance themselves then they probably know more than they're letting on.'

'It looks like Alfred Smith has dashed off as well,' said Philip, glancing around. 'Not exactly chatty here, are they? Apart from this lady though.'

Mrs Evans waved as she approached. 'Hello, Detective! How are you getting on with your investigation?'

'This is Mrs Evans,' Philip said to Augusta. 'She was a neighbour of Mr Trigwell's.'

'What a sad day indeed,' she said. 'And I must say I'm sad there was a low attendance too. It seems Robert didn't have many friends. Still, I suppose he liked it that way. Not everyone wants a lot of friends, do they? Have you come here to see if the murderer is attending?'

'I'm not sure if any of the attendees could be the murderer, Mrs Evans. But we're certainly interested in seeing who turned up to pay their respects,' said Philip. 'You're right that Mr Trigwell didn't appear to have many friends and, in fact, we've struggled to find many people who knew him well.'

'I imagine you've spoken to his sister?'

'We have.'

'And there's her man friend too.'

'Do you know what he's called?'

'Douglas Robson, apparently. I saw you speaking to the J Baker man just now, Simon Granger. He had little to say for himself. I spoke briefly to that young man, he appears to have left already. James Godwin. Apparently, he was a friend of Robert's from the war.'

'James?'

'Yes.'

'Are you sure that's what he said?'

'Oh yes. Have you spoken to him yet?'

Philip paused before replying, clearly choosing a tactful response. 'Not yet. But I'll make sure that we do.'

Chapter 25

'WELL THAT WENT AS WELL as it could have done, don't you think, darling?' Douglas escorted Isabella to her usual chair. 'Cigarette?'

'Thank you.' She took one from the packet he offered and he held out his lighter for her.

'I'm going to make a complaint to Scotland Yard,' said Annie.

'Oh, I'm quite sure there's no need.' Isabella inhaled on her cigarette and rubbed her aching head. She felt exhausted.

'Yes, there is a need!' said Annie. 'It's disrespectful! The police shouldn't be hanging about at funerals.'

'They kept their distance,' said Isabella. 'And I'm glad they didn't speak to me. I can only imagine they were on the lookout for the killer.'

Douglas laughed. 'As if a murderer would attend the victim's funeral! What nonsense. Sadly, I think it's going to be some time before they catch the culprit.'

'I shall make some tea,' said Annie.

'I need something stronger,' said Isabella. 'Can we have

sherry?'

'Alright then.' Annie smiled and went off to make the drinks.

Douglas stood in the centre of the room, his legs planted in a wide stance and his hands in his pockets. He seemed restless. She wanted him to sit down.

'You must rattle around in here like a dried pea in a barrel,' he said.

Isabella glared at him. 'You're describing me as a dried pea?'

He laughed. 'Only for a bit of fun, darling. What I meant by it is that this place is too large for you now, wouldn't you say?'

'I know what you meant by it. And no, I don't consider it too large. It's a nice size.'

'Properties in Chelsea are overpriced now.'

'I wouldn't know.'

'People are willing to pay a very good price for a place like this. More than it's worth, I'd say. You've got an excellent opportunity to capitalise on that.'

She blew a cloud of smoke at him. 'You think I should sell this flat?' It seemed too soon after Robert's death to be considering such a thing.

'It's the sensible thing to do. And besides, it must be full of sad memories for you.'

'Why sad?'

'Because you lived here with your mother and now she's no longer around.'

'Most of my memories in this flat are happy ones. And besides, Mother wouldn't have wanted me to sell it.'

Douglas hitched his trousers at the knee and sat on the red sofa. 'But she's no longer here. Surely what she would, or wouldn't, have wanted is irrelevant?'

His words stung. 'Douglas! How dare you? I knew my

mother far better than you ever did. I know that she would have been extremely upset to ever lose this flat.'

'Selling it is not the same as losing it. And wouldn't she have wanted you to be happy? If you sold this flat and found happiness with the money you made from it, surely she would have been pleased about that?'

'She would have wanted Robert to be happy, too. Thank goodness she didn't live long enough to experience his fate.'

'Yes, that's a blessing. And it shows that no matter what people want from life, there's no guarantee it will happen. It's time to think about what you want, darling. For the first time in your life, you have freedom. Isn't that wonderful?'

'It doesn't feel like freedom,' she said. 'There's too much to sort out.'

He took her hand. 'Of course it doesn't at the moment. You're going through a difficult time, Issy. But soon the clouds will pass and the sun will come out to shine again. There's no harm in making a few plans now so that you can fully enjoy your life when you're ready to.'

She pulled her hand away. 'I feel like you're rushing me to make decisions.'

'Oh no, darling, I'm not doing that at all! I'm sorry you feel that way, it certainly wasn't my intention. I suppose I just want to make sure you have a plan for the future. Sometimes, when people are grieving, they get lost in it and they get stuck in a rut and never seem to find their way out. Years later, they then have regrets about what they could have done. I just want to make sure that you can view everything with clarity.' He took her hand again and lowered his voice. 'I just want you to know I'm here for you. I'm by your side.'

'And your wife?'

'We're getting a divorce. I've told you that.'

She looked him in the eye. 'I need evidence.'

He smiled. 'I know you're upset at the moment, Issy. But isn't my word enough?'

'Sometimes I think you tell me what you want me to hear. Have you actually petitioned for divorce?'

'I'm meeting my solicitor this week.' He squeezed her hand. 'This is a difficult time, but everything is going to get better. I promise.'

Chapter 26

'I'm sorry darling, but I have a confession,' said Douglas. 'No, that won't do. Confession is the wrong word to use... I'm sorry darling, but I'm going to ask my solicitor for a divorce.' The word hung in his mind as he drove through Bayswater en route from Chelsea to his home in Willesden.

Divorce.

He could picture Diana's face crumpling as he mentioned the word. How could he bring himself to say it? And should he tell her about Isabella? Or should he just pretend that he had fallen out of love with her? Both reasons were hurtful.

He reasoned he had to tell Diana about Isabella because they were going to get engaged as soon as the divorce was completed. There was no use in telling her any more lies. It was about time he came clean.

But it was going to be so difficult! And what about Diana's parents? What were they going to say? His hands tightened around the steering wheel as he thought of the drama which was going to ensue.

He had to think about the money instead. Isabella was

rich! It was a shame the solicitor couldn't tell her the value of Robert's estate yet, but Douglas estimated her Chelsea flat was worth about five thousand. Over ten times the salary he had earned as an insurance clerk! And that was just the flat. The furnishings were worth a lot, too. He felt sure he could persuade her to sell all of it. Why would she want to live in a place which reminded her of her dead mother every day?

They could sell the place, then travel. A cruise around the Mediterranean to begin with, then a trip to Egypt and the holy lands. Now that Robert's funeral was over, he planned to make these suggestions to Isabella. He felt sure the ideas would excite her.

But he had to get divorced, and that was going to make things uncomfortable for a while. He had told Isabella that he and Diana were estranged, but that had been a little lie to keep Isabella happy. Diana had no idea that he was planning to leave at all. What a pickle!

He drove across the bridge over the railway lines at Royal Oak and reached the junction with Harrow Road. He prepared to turn left, but then thought of the King's Head pub close by. A drink or two before he spoke to Diana wouldn't hurt. He turned the steering wheel and went right.

Chapter 27

'So the Westminster Abbey cloister killer hasn't been caught yet?' asked Lady Hereford, as she fed birdseed to Sparky.

'Not yet,' said Augusta.

'Cloister killer,' said Fred. 'I like that phrase. I'm surprised the newspapers haven't used that one yet.'

'They can't now,' said Lady Hereford. 'Because I made it up.'

'It's proving difficult to catch the murderer,' said Augusta. 'We've found out so little about Robert Trigwell. He's clearly got caught up in something, but we don't yet know what.'

'Well perhaps you've got nowhere with the case, but I can tell you've done good work with Sparky.'

'Have I?'

'Yes. He's not snatching his seeds at all today! You've clearly been disciplining him very well.'

Augusta and Fred exchanged a glance, both knowing Augusta had done nothing different.

A stooped, grey-haired man entered the shop. 'Do you have any poetry collections?' he asked.

'Yes,' replied Augusta. 'They're on the upstairs floor.'

The old man thanked her and began to climb the staircase.

'I can say with certainty that Sparky's behaviour has improved dramatically,' continued Lady Hereford. 'He's almost a different canary entirely. You haven't swapped him, have you?'

Augusta laughed. 'I could never swap Sparky. He's completely unique.'

'He certainly is,' said Lady Hereford. 'A fine young canary indeed.'

A loud cry from the mezzanine floor above interrupted them.

'What on earth was that?' said Augusta, dashing out from behind the counter. She ran up the stairs, two at a time, and found the elderly customer half-sitting on the floor. He was being helped to his feet by a man with dark hair and a thin moustache. Augusta rushed over to assist.

'What happened?'

'He frightened the living daylights out of me!' said the old man. 'I was just looking through the poetry section when he appeared from nowhere and scared me half to death!'

'I do apologise,' said the man.

'And so you should!' snapped Augusta. 'You can't frighten my customers like this!'

'I'm sorry.'

'Why do you keep walking through my shop?'

'To get to and from my office.'

'I gathered that. But why walk through my shop when you can use the door on the street?'

'It's quicker. This door here leads directly to my office.

But if I use the door on the street, then I have to walk along a corridor and through the secretarial office.'

'So you'd rather walk through my shop instead?'

'Yes.'

'I can't permit you to use my shop as a through route. It's private property, and this gentleman has been frightened by your sudden appearance.'

'I've apologised for it.'

'That may be so. But there's a risk you'll scare other customers too. Your business premises are separate from mine and I request that this door be kept locked at all times and that you don't use my shop for access.'

He sighed. 'It's going to be rather inconvenient for me.'

'And it's inconvenient for me having you coming and going through my shop as you please! Who's in charge of your firm?'

'Two people are in charge. Mr Fitzwilliam and Mr Harper.'

'I think I shall have to speak to them about it.'

'There's no need. I shall use the longer route in future.'

Fred made some tea for the elderly customer and Augusta encouraged him to take a seat by the counter to recover.

'It's a disgrace,' said Lady Hereford. 'People should be able to peacefully browse bookshops without being frightened to death. Do you want me to speak to the landlord, Sir Pritchard, about it, Augusta?'

'Thank you for the offer, Lady Hereford, but there's no need to mention it to him. I'm hoping that the staff in the bookkeeping firm have learned their lesson after this.'

'I thought he was a ghost!' said the elderly customer. 'And I don't even believe in ghosts.'

'Don't you?' said Lady Hereford. 'I believe in them.

I'm quite convinced the ghost of my late husband haunts me.'

'Really?'

'Oh yes!'

Augusta smiled as Lady Hereford embarked on a ghost story and the elderly customer listened open-mouthed.

The telephone rang and Augusta answered it.

'I'm afraid it's me again,' said Philip. 'Are you tired of me yet?'

'Very tired.'

He laughed. 'Alright then, I'll keep this quick. I've arranged to meet a chap at the East Surrey Regiment tomorrow who knew both Trigwell and Smith. I want to learn more about the mysterious pair. Would you like to join me?'

'Yes.'

'Wonderful.'

Chapter 28

SYLVIA ARRIVED ten minutes late at Baker's Tea Rooms on Oxford Street. She slumped in her chair and gave Alfred a sad look.

'How are you?' he asked, preparing himself for a difficult conversation. Sylvia had sent him a telegram asking to meet, but the pair had not spoken since the Scotland Yard detective and his assistant had turned up on the riverside by St Thomas's. It had been pure bad luck that Alfred had been with Sylvia at the time. If she hadn't turned up, then she would have been oblivious to his friendship with Robert Trigwell. But instead, he had to placate her.

'How do you think I am?' she replied.

'I'm sorry, Sylvia. I never intended to upset you.'

'Your secrecy worries me, Alfred. Why didn't you tell me you knew the man who was murdered in Westminster Abbey?'

'Because it was a tragic event which I didn't really want to talk about. It saddens me.'

'But I feel you purposefully kept it from me.'

'I didn't. I just didn't tell anyone. And besides, if I had mentioned him to you, then you'd have asked me lots of questions about him.'

'And what's wrong with that?'

'I knew him during the war. And I don't like talking about the war. You know that. I have a new life now. We all do. There's no use in thinking about the past.'

'I may have asked you questions, but you could have told me you didn't want to talk about the war. I'd have much preferred you did that rather than pretend you didn't know him.'

'I didn't pretend! I just didn't mention it. I'm sorry if it upset you, it certainly wasn't my intention. I wasn't keeping anything from you.'

Sylvia wrapped her pink scarf a little tighter around her neck and folded her arms. Alfred caught a waitress's attention and ordered two teas. Then he continued, 'And besides, we don't all tell each other everything about ourselves, do we? I'm sure there are things you don't tell me. And I'm not saying they're secrets or anything important, they're just things which you keep to yourself.'

'I tell you everything, Alfred!'

'I see.' He sighed. Sylvia wasn't coming round to his way of thinking.

'I like to share everything with you!' she said.

'Alright. But not everyone is the same. You will meet some people in life who like to talk about everything, much like you, Sylvia. And you will meet other people in life who prefer to be a little more private. It doesn't mean they're being deceptive, it's just the way they prefer to be. We're all different, Sylvia, and I think our relationship could become difficult if we expect certain things from each other.'

'Surely there has to be some expectation?'

'Yes, some. But we also have to accept our differences.'

'I'm not sure if I can trust you,' she said. Her eyes grew moist. 'Even though you tell me you have nothing to hide, I feel wary. I wish I didn't! I keep thinking about how everyone has been talking about the murder in Westminster Abbey and yet you couldn't bring yourself to mention you knew the victim! I understand people don't tell each other everything, but it seems such an odd piece of information to withhold. And I'm wondering now if Father has seen something in you which I haven't.'

His stomach clenched. 'Such as what?'

'When I asked him why he refused to approve of our engagement, he told me he knew what was best for me. He's said that sort of thing before and I've just dismissed him as a silly old-fashioned fool who worries too much about me. But now I wonder if his instincts are right. Does he really know you're not the right husband for me? Should I trust his instincts rather than mine?'

Alfred shifted uncomfortably in his chair. Sylvia had clearly been giving everything a lot of thought. He realised he had been foolish not to mention he knew Robert, but he hadn't imagined her ever finding out he had known him. All he could do now was persuade her that he would be a loving and caring husband.

The waitress brought their tea. When she left, he leant forward and tried to be as persuasive as possible. 'I truly love you, Sylvia, and I'd do anything for you. I accept you completely. I can only hope you accept me for who I am. Your father is protective of you, and that's understandable. If we have a daughter together, then I shall feel the same about her.'

'So, is he being too protective?'

'Yes, I think he is. I wonder if your father is the sort of man who would disapprove of any suitor.'

'I suppose he would be cautious of most men. But I don't know… I suppose I'm wary now because he doesn't approve of you and then I found out you kept information from me.'

How he wished he could make her forget about it! 'It wasn't information which was important to us though, was it? It had nothing to do with our engagement. It was just someone I knew in the past and I've already explained why I didn't wish to talk about it.' He flung himself back in his chair. 'I really don't know what else I can do to persuade you, Sylvia. What more can I say? Do you want us to marry or not?'

'I don't know.'

He felt nauseous. He didn't want to lose Sylvia. He couldn't imagine meeting another woman like her. He felt sure they could be happy together, but the combination of her father's disapproval and the discovery of a friendship he hadn't mentioned was worrying her. The timing was unfortunate. Even after her father's rebuff, she had been happy to continue the relationship. But now she was not so sure.

Perhaps she was more perceptive than he had given her credit for? Perhaps he had been hiding for so long that he had become complacent and shown hints of his true self. Perhaps the truth was emerging, no matter how hard he tried to control it. Like weeds in a carefully tended flower bed.

He felt a flush of heat in his face. The burning of shame.

And now he felt like she could see through his skin and see into him. See him for who he really was.

'Alfred?'

He felt an urgent need to get away.

'Are you alright?'

He got to his feet and pulled his coat from the back of his chair. 'You clearly need more time to think about this, Sylvia. Please let me know when you've made a decision.'

'Alfred?!'

He bolted for the door.

Chapter 29

THE EAST SURREY Regiment barracks were in Kingston-upon-Thames, a town which was a thirty-minute train journey from Waterloo station.

'How nice to be out of the dirt and smoke of London,' said Philip as they walked towards the barracks. It was a fresh March day and bright yellow daffodils brightened the gardens of the houses they passed. 'Although at the rate London's spreading, Kingston will probably be swallowed up by it soon enough.'

The entrance block for the barracks was an austere brick building with three square turrets. Once admitted, they were shown to Captain Lowther's office. It was a spartan, pristine room which smelt of boot polish.

'Private Trigwell and Private Smith?' he said. His red hair was fading to grey, and he had a strong jaw and sharp grey eyes. 'Yes, I remember them. They served in my platoon in Carnoy. Brave men, the pair of them. I was saddened to read about Trigwell's death.'

'They were friends?' asked Philip.

'They were indeed.' He held Philip's gaze as if there was more to say, but he wasn't going to volunteer it.

'We've spoken to Alfred Smith recently,' said Philip.

'And how is he faring these days?'

'He appears to be well. He's a medical student.'

'Is he?' Captain Lowther raised an eyebrow. 'Good for him. Many men have struggled with adjusting to normal life again. It was never a problem for me because I'm still here.' He smiled. 'I enrolled in the regular army in 1909. Military service is all I've ever known.'

'We've asked Alfred Smith about his friendship with Robert Trigwell,' said Philip. 'And he's tight-lipped about it.'

'I suppose he has the right to be. Many men are - as you put it - tight-lipped about their wartime experiences. There's no use in reliving it, is there?' He sat back and surveyed Philip. 'I won't ask you your age, sir, but were you enrolled?'

'I worked in intelligence during the war.'

'How interesting! Sometimes you chaps made our lives easier, sometimes you made them harder.' He chuckled. 'It's all water under the bridge now, I suppose.'

'Mrs Peel and I worked in intelligence together during the war.'

'Is that so?' He gave Augusta a smile. 'Then I commend you both.'

'Let's return to Smith and Trigwell,' said Philip. 'We've established they were friends during the war and both led quiet, private lives afterwards. Smith told us he hadn't seen Trigwell since the war and it seems Trigwell was keen to find him.' Philip explained how Trigwell had visited Augusta and asked her to find a long-lost friend. 'We're assuming the long-lost friend was Smith because Trigwell gave a nurse his name shortly before he died. What he didn't know at the time was that the man he sought was in the same hospital.'

'Goodness. What were the chances of that, eh?'

'Mr Trigwell gave me a false name, initially,' said Augusta. 'He told me his name was Symes.'

'That rings a bell,' said Captain Lowther. 'Trigwell was called Symes for some reason.'

'Smith said he came up with the name because Trigwell reminded him of a friend from school.'

'Is that the reason? You know what it's like, someone comes up with a name for another chap and before long everyone's using it.'

'I'm hoping you might shed some more light on their friendship, Captain,' said Philip.

'Shed some light?' He picked up a pipe and began filling it with tobacco from a little tin. 'I don't know about that. I didn't know them well. But they were good soldiers.'

'I sense there's something you're not telling me.'

'I don't like to speak ill of the men who fought so bravely for our country.'

'But?'

'I suppose you have a murder to investigate and so I shall speak directly.'

They waited while he lit his pipe. Then he sat back in his chair with the pipe in his mouth. 'There were... rumours about Smith and Trigwell. I'm sure you don't need me to explain any further than that.'

'Do you think there was truth behind the rumours?'

'I don't know for sure. But the rumours didn't surprise me. Both chaps were a little different to your average chap, but there was no evidence of their homosexuality. If there had been, they would have been court-martialled and sent home. Once back home, they could have been tried for indecency in a civilian court and sentenced to hard labour.'

Augusta began to understand the pair's desperation for secrecy.

'I reiterate that both Smith and Trigwell were good, brave soldiers,' said Captain Lowther. 'They showed no cowardice and did everything required of them. They weren't the only men of their ilk and, with no evidence of any deviance, the best any of us could do was just get on with the job at hand. They were risking their lives as much as the next man. As far as I'm aware, neither was promoted above the rank of private. They deserved to be promoted, but the more disagreeable elements of their character held them back. I find it rather interesting that you're here speaking to me today.'

'Why's that?' asked Philip.

'I was contacted recently by an old friend of mine, a retired colonel. He was enquiring about Alfred Smith.'

'What did he want to know?'

'The original question came from a gentleman at the colonel's club. As I understand it, the gentleman's daughter was courting Smith, and he was interested in knowing more about the chap.'

'What did you tell the retired colonel?'

'I told him what I've just told you. As a father myself, I would want to be informed of such things.'

'How do you think the father of the young woman would have received the news?'

'Impossible to say. I don't know who he was. Just a friend of a friend.'

'But based on what you told the colonel, do you think the father would have been happy for his daughter to continue her relationship with Smith?'

He sighed. 'You're asking me to guess and I can't speak

for someone else. But if I were the father receiving such a report about a chap my daughter was courting, I'd be extremely reluctant for the relationship to continue.'

A short while later, Philip and Augusta walked back to Kingston-upon-Thames railway station.

'So I think we know now why Sylvia Golding's father didn't approve of the planned marriage,' she said.

'Absolutely,' said Philip.

'But a rumour is still a rumour until there's evidence. Captain Lowther said himself there was no evidence of the men's homosexuality.'

'It may have been just a rumour. But how else do you explain the men's secrecy? And Trigwell was keen to find Smith again. Presumably Smith wanted nothing more to do with him? Instead, he wanted to lead what he considered a respectable married life.'

'And I suppose it's interesting that Trigwell didn't marry, nor is there any sign that he ever intended to. Instead, he led a quiet bachelor's existence. I wonder if he had been trying to contact Smith for a while and Smith ignored him. And I can understand now why Smith didn't tell Miss Golding about his friendship with Trigwell. Perhaps he worried she would find out about their closeness and call off the marriage.'

'So there's a possibility Trigwell was a threat to Smith's future plans and happiness? That's an interesting theory to consider.'

Chapter 30

'THE NEXT APPOINTMENT I have today is with the Trigwell family's solicitor,' said Philip as the train took them back to Waterloo. 'He's requested to meet with me.'

'Why?'

'I don't know, but it will be an excellent opportunity to find out what he knows about Robert Trigwell. You're very welcome to come with me, Augusta, if you're happy to leave Fred in charge of the shop for a little longer.'

'I'm always happy to leave him in charge. In fact, everything seems to run a little smoother when I'm not there.' Augusta told Philip about the problem she was having with the new tenants in the offices above the shop.

'Oh dear,' he said. 'They don't sound very considerate. If you'd like a Scotland Yard detective to have a strong word with them, I'll be happy to oblige.'

Augusta laughed. 'Hopefully it won't come to that.'

'Just a moment... Could one of those people have crept behind your counter and found the note which Robert Trigwell gave to you?'

'I doubt it.'

'But there's a possibility.'

'I suppose there is. But how would they know what the note referred to?'

'Perhaps they overhead your conversation?'

'But why would they wish to murder him?'

'I don't know.'

'And the note hadn't been moved since I'd placed it on the shelf under the counter. I really don't think one of the bookkeepers found it, read it, put it back exactly where it was, and then murdered Robert Trigwell.'

'Fair enough,' said Philip. 'But we should bear them in mind if we get nowhere with our other lines of enquiry. Fancy strolling through your shop with no consideration. Some people can be rather strange. In fact, I encountered a strange person yesterday evening.'

'Who?'

'An old schoolfriend of mine. The chap my wife had an affair with. Can you believe it? It was the last thing I needed after a busy day.'

'He called on you?' Augusta could scarcely believe what she was hearing.

'Yes, he had the audacity to turn up and tell me how sorry he was.'

'Why did he do that?'

'I really don't know. A guilty conscience, perhaps? I think he was hoping I'd forgive him so he could feel better about his actions. The affair has ended now.'

'So what did you say to him?'

'I told him to clear off.'

'Good.'

'I said I had nothing to say to him, nor did I want to hear his feeble explanation for conducting an affair with my wife. It's astonishing how sorry people are when they're caught out, isn't it? They're happy to indulge themselves with no care for how their actions hurt other people, and when everyone finds out, they're full of repentance. I've no time for people like that.'

'Me neither.'

'They're selfish people. Only interested in themselves.'

'I agree.'

'So I hope he continues to feel bad about what he's done. Hopefully for the rest of his days. Does that make me seem rather bitter?'

'No. Not at all. He helped end your marriage and break up your family.'

'It's interesting that you use the word *helped*. It wasn't entirely his fault. My wife has to share some of the blame. As do I.'

'Why you?'

'I wasn't as attentive as I should have been.'

'I'm sure you were.'

'I wasn't. It's the job I do. It tires me out.'

'That's not surprising. The hours can be long and unpredictable.'

'Even so, it shouldn't be used as an excuse to neglect my family.'

'I'm sure you didn't *neglect* them!'

'I didn't make enough time for them. It's easy to blame work and other demands, but it was my responsibility to ensure I didn't allow other aspects of my life to take over. And I'm afraid I did. Audrey got fed up with me and had an affair with someone else.'

'I think she should have discussed it with you. It was wrong for her to go off with someone else.'

'The trouble is, she tried to discuss it with me. But I was tired and grumpy and not very receptive. I look back now and realise the warning was there. I didn't do enough to address it. I took her for granted and look where it's got me. The reality is I'm quite a grumpy, self-centred individual and I realise now I'm probably not much fun to be married to.'

'Oh Philip! You're being much too hard on yourself!'

'I'm afraid it's the truth.'

'No it's not! I don't find you grumpy or self-centred.'

'That's because you're not married to me, Augusta. I do a good job of presenting myself well to the rest of the world, but at home I'm a curmudgeon.'

'So why do you think that is?'

'Who knows? The war? Although it's over, it's left its shadow in all of us. And I'm reminded of that when we speak to other people about it. We've all done our best to pretend the horror never happened, but that doesn't make it go away, does it?'

'No. It won't ever go away. And we're all entitled to feel sad and upset. It doesn't make you a curmudgeon, Philip. You're just a normal human being.'

'Those are kind words, Augusta. And it's very honourable of you to believe my grumpiness is normal. You may change your mind if you're ever at the receiving end of it.'

'I wouldn't mind.'

'Oh, I refuse to believe that.' He turned to the window. 'Looks like we're coming into Waterloo.'

Chapter 31

Mr Barrington welcomed Augusta and Philip in the plush Belgravia offices of Barrington, Harris and Wilson.

'Thank you for coming to see me,' he said, as he seated his plump frame behind his large mahogany desk. 'I have a concern I'd like to speak to you about, but there is a possibility it's entirely unfounded.'

'But it's a concern nonetheless,' said Philip. 'So it's important to share it.'

'That's what I thought. I've been the solicitor for the Trigwell family for a number of years. Mr Hugo Trigwell and his wife, and old Mr Marmaduke Trigwell before them. He lived to a ripe old age. These days, of course, my client is Miss Isabella Trigwell. And sadly she's the last of them.'

They were interrupted for a few minutes while a woman in a white apron and cap wheeled in a trolley and served them tea.

'Thank you, Mrs Perkins,' said Mr Barrington. 'Now where was I?'

'You have concerns,' said Philip.

'Yes, I do indeed. The gentleman I'm concerned about is Mr Douglas Robson. He's... I'm not actually sure what he is, really. Miss Trigwell tells me he's a friend of hers but, from what I've seen of them, he seems a little too friendly for a friend. And I'm sure Miss Trigwell told me he's married. I first met him, in the company of Miss Trigwell, after her mother's death. But ever since the death of her brother, Mr Robson has been present at every meeting. He's taking a keen interest in the family estate.'

'Does Miss Trigwell inherit the estate?' asked Augusta.

'She does. Her brother didn't leave a will, and she's his closest relative. We're in the process of valuing the estate at the moment and it's taking a little while.'

'Is it worth a lot?'

'Yes, it is.'

'Are you able to give us a rough idea of how much?' asked Philip.

'Well, there's a bit of work to do yet, but we suspect the entire estate could be in the region of twenty-five thousand pounds.'

'Good grief.'

Augusta couldn't imagine what it would be like to inherit that much money. The income from her bookshop paid her a salary of two hundred and fifty pounds a year.

'Mr Robson is a man who has only recently become acquainted with Miss Trigwell,' said Mr Barrington. 'And I think he's taking an unnatural interest in the estate. To put it bluntly, I think he's after the money. I've had to make the difficult decision of asking her to not involve him in our meetings. I made up some nonsense about it being a legal requirement.'

'That sounds very sensible.'

'Miss Trigwell needs protecting. I'm concerned because she's experienced two bereavements within a short space of time. I worry the upset has impaired her judgment. And now her brother has died, she is a wealthy woman. I worry she might fall prey to a charming gentleman like Mr Robson. Perhaps I have misinterpreted his intentions, and he's merely excited for her, but I can't help thinking that his enthusiasm is based on a hope that he'll personally benefit from the death of her family members.'

'What's your general opinion of the man?' asked Augusta.

'I don't know him well. But he appears to be a married man who's taking a keen interest in a wealthy, unmarried lady. Make of that what you will.'

'Do you think he could be a murderer?' asked Philip.

'Goodness! I couldn't possibly say! Are you referring to the murder of Robert Trigwell?'

'Yes. Do you think Douglas Robson could have attacked him?'

'I simply couldn't speculate on that. I merely wanted to inform you of my concerns, Detective Inspector. I admit I don't warm to the chap, but it doesn't mean he's a murderer.'

'I apologise for putting you on the spot like that, Mr Barrington,' said Philip. 'I suppose I'm interested to get your impression of the man. I've not met him properly myself but I think it's about time I acquainted myself with him. It seems to me there's a possibility he's befriended Miss Trigwell with an evil scheme in mind.'

'The murder of her brother and a share in the fortune?'

'It's a possible motive isn't it? Just a theory though. I sometimes wonder if I've worked on too many of these cases and am merely determined to see the bad in everyone.'

'It's your job to consider all possibilities, Detective Inspector.'

'Yes, it is. Thank you for speaking with us. And if you notice anything else unusual or suspicious, you'll let me know, won't you?'

'I certainly will.'

Chapter 32

Simon Granger sat at his desk in the offices of J Baker and looked out of the window. He was watching the shapely shop manager across the road rearrange her window display again. The mannequins were dressed in new outfits every week. This week, their stylish dresses were pastel pink and yellow, and the shop manager was positioning colourful paper flowers at their feet. A spring meadow in the centre of London. Simon decided he would visit the shop later and compliment the manager on her new display. Perhaps he could finally persuade her to go for a drink with him.

A knock at his office door interrupted his thoughts. A young, sandy-haired man stepped into the room.

'What is it, Lewis?'

'I can't find the file.'

'Which one?'

'*The* file.'

'Have you looked properly?'

'Yes. It's not there.'

Simon felt his heart thud a little faster. He tried to reassure himself there was nothing to worry about and pressed the buzzer on his desk for his secretary, Miss Haynes.

She arrived in his office moments later. 'Yes, sir?'

'Have you seen the Whittaker file?' he asked.

'I believe it's on Mr Baker's desk.'

His heart thudded even faster, but he did his best to remain calm.

'Do you know what he wants with it?'

'No. He was looking through the filing cabinet yesterday and—'

'He was looking through the filing cabinet?' Mr Baker never looked through the files himself. He usually asked someone else to do it for him.

'Yes, sir.'

'And he took the Whittaker file?'

'Yes. Is there a problem?'

'No. It's just such a small, inconsequential file that I don't know why he'd be interested in it. Lewis here was looking for it just now, you see.'

'Right. Well, I can ask Mr Baker if he's finished with it if you need it?'

'No, it's quite alright, Miss Haynes. At least we've solved the mystery now.' He dismissed them both from his office with a wave.

He looked out of the window again. There was no sign of the shapely shop manager anymore. Had Robert Trigwell told Mr Baker about the file before his death? Simon had assumed not. But why was Mr Baker interested in it? It was kept tucked away at the back of the filing cabinet. How had Mr Baker known it was there?

He thought back to the day when Robert Trigwell had stood in this office and asked him about the Whittaker file. The man had been his junior, and yet he'd had the nerve to confront him!

Robert had entered his office with a neatly documented list of amounts which didn't tally. He had asked for an explanation of each one, and Simon had calmly responded. But he had watched Robert's face grow hostile as it became apparent that money was missing, and Simon was responsible for it. He had explained away a few mistakes, but Robert had found dozens.

Simon had made no mistakes in the early months, everything had balanced perfectly. It had seemed so easy. As his confidence had grown, so had the amounts of money. His teeth clenched with anger as he thought about how careless he had become.

He had been sure that all the amounts tallied up. An amount entered into one column had to balance an amount in another column, that was the golden rule. As long as everything had balanced, he had been fine. But Robert had found an amount which hadn't. Then he had found another. Then another.

Robert had led such a quiet life that he'd had time to discover other people's mistakes. There had been no distractions for him. No wife and children making demands on his time. The meagre attendance at the funeral showed that he'd had very few friends. His only hobby appeared to have been reading. A quiet, solitary pursuit which required no interaction with others. Simon gave a dry laugh as he thought about the dull existence Robert had led. He'd had little to think about and lots of time to go through the ledgers. He had probably taken them home with him and worked on them during the evenings.

The meeting with Robert that day hadn't ended well. Simon had run out of explanations and Robert had informed him it was his duty to report his suspicions to Mr Baker.

That's when Simon had threatened him.

He had assumed the threat had worked. But had Robert reported his findings to Mr Baker, regardless?

Robert Trigwell was still causing trouble for him. Even two weeks after his death.

Chapter 33

PHILIP WAS ALREADY WAITING for Augusta when she stepped out of Sloane Square tube station the following morning.

'It will be interesting to hear what Isabella Trigwell tells us about Douglas Robson, won't it?' he said as they walked to the flat in Sloane Court. 'Detective Sergeant Joyce is meeting us there. I got into trouble yesterday.'

'What happened?'

'The commissioner told me off for not including his precious son in our interviews with the captain and the solicitor.'

'But that's ridiculous!'

'Not if you're the commissioner. He wants his son to learn all about conducting a murder investigation.'

'Can't Joyce spend time with another detective instead?'

'The Trigwell case is the most interesting one the Yard is dealing with at the moment. It's no wonder the commissioner wants his son involved.'

'How infuriating.'

'It certainly is.'

. . .

Detective Sergeant Joyce greeted them with a cheery smile outside Miss Trigwell's apartment block. 'Good morning!' he said, rubbing his hands together. 'Are we ready to do business?'

'I think so, Joyce,' said Philip. 'Now don't forget you're here to learn. Please listen to the questions I ask rather than rushing in with your own.'

'Yes, sir. Understood.'

Mrs Hargreaves, the housekeeper, admitted them to the flat. 'Please make this quick,' she said. 'Miss Trigwell is tired. If you upset her, I'll wring your necks.'

Augusta felt this threat was uncalled for as they followed Mrs Hargreaves into the sitting room. Isabella Trigwell sat smoking a cigarette in her usual leather chair.

'You're here to update me on progress?' she asked.

'Actually, we have a few more questions,' said Philip.

'So there's been no progress?'

'We have a few suspects in mind,' said Detective Sergeant Joyce. Philip gave him a sharp look.

'Who?' asked Miss Trigwell.

'We need to ask you some questions first,' said Philip. He pointed at a red velvet chair. 'Sit down there, Joyce, please.' Then he took a seat next to Augusta on the red sofa. 'What can you tell us about Douglas Robson?' He asked Miss Trigwell.

Her scarlet lips raised into a smile. 'He's a friend of mine.'

'A romantic friend?'

'Yes. We've been courting for a few months.'

'Where did you meet?'

'At a dance.'

'I apologise for the bluntness of my next question,' said

Philip. 'But I have to ask it. Has Mr Robson proposed marriage to you?'

Miss Trigwell smiled again. 'No. But that's because there's a small hurdle at the moment. He's actually already married. Although he and his wife have been estranged for some time. He's currently divorcing her.'

'So the pair of you can marry?'

She inhaled on her cigarette. 'That's right. I know what it looks like, Detective Inspector, but we're not all perfect, you know.'

'I wasn't passing judgement, Miss Trigwell. I'm merely interested in the nature of your relationship with him.'

'Why?'

'You're a wealthy woman, so I hope his intentions are honourable.'

'Of course they are!'

The housekeeper brought in a tray with a teapot, cups and a fruit cake on it.

'Oh lovely, Annie, thank you,' said Miss Trigwell. 'Just what we need.'

'We need to speak to Mr Robson,' said Philip. 'Where does he live?'

'Why do you need to speak to him?'

'We're speaking to everyone who knew your brother.'

'But he and Robert barely knew each other!'

'Even so, I should like to speak with him.'

'He lives in Willesden. Annie will write the address down for you in a moment, won't you, Annie?'

'Of course,' replied the housekeeper, pouring out the tea.

'Where does he work?' Augusta asked.

'Goodness, you really are interested in him all of a sudden, aren't you? He works at a private bank in the City. Albemarle and Forester.'

'Is he there at the moment?'

'Yes, I imagine so.'

'What does Mr Robson think about your newly inherited wealth?' asked Philip.

'I don't think he's given it much thought.'

'Really?'

'Yes. He's been supporting me with the death of my mother and brother. There's been little time to think of anything else.'

'And you've found him supportive?'

'Enormously. He and Annie have kept me going these past few weeks. I don't know what I'd do without them.'

'That's good to hear.'

Mrs Hargreaves handed out plates with thick slices of fruitcake on them. Detective Sergeant Joyce wasted no time tucking into his. Augusta took a bite and found it so rich and sweet that she wasn't sure she could finish it.

'I hope you don't mind me asking this, Miss Trigwell, but it's a question we're asking everyone,' said Philip. 'Can you tell me where you were on the night of your brother's death?'

'I was here.'

'And can anyone vouch for that?'

'Of course.' She turned to her housekeeper. 'Annie, where was I on the night that Robert died?'

'You were here, Miss Trigwell.'

'Thank you,' said Philip. 'All evening?'

'Yes,' said Mrs Hargreaves. 'All evening. And then Mr Robson called round.'

'What time was that?'

'Eight o'clock I think.'

'Does that answer your question, Detective Inspector?' asked Miss Trigwell.

'It does. Thank you.'

Chapter 34

'WHAT DO THEY WANT WITH DOUGLAS?' Isabella asked Annie once the Scotland Yard detectives and Mrs Peel had left. 'Do they suspect him of something?'

'I imagine they must do.'

'I should warn him. I don't understand why they're pestering us when they should be out there looking for Robert's killer. They never answered my question about their progress, did they?'

'The young detective said they had some suspects.'

'And from the way they're talking, it sounds like they suspect Douglas. Could they really think he'd murder Robert?'

'They've not caught anyone yet, so they must be getting desperate.'

The doorbell interrupted them and Isabella's heart sank.

'Oh no, that's not them again, is it?'

'Let me go and see.'

Annie returned to the room with a gentleman in a pinstriped suit. His hair was slicked back, and he held a paper file under one arm.

'This is Mr Wright,' said Annie. 'He's an estate agent.'

'Mrs Robson?' he said, holding out his hand.

'I beg your pardon?'

He withdrew his hand. 'You're not Mrs Robson?'

'I'm Miss Trigwell.'

'I see. I apologise for any confusion. Mr Robson visited my office yesterday and asked about a valuation of this property. We didn't make any firm arrangements at the time, but I was passing just now and thought I'd call with a view to discussing it further.' Isabella watched him cast his eye appreciatively over the room. 'The properties in this building are very popular. Mr Robson will find himself with quite a queue of willing buyers.'

'This is not Mr Robson's flat,' she said. 'It's mine.'

'Oh, I do apologise! I hope you forgive my mistake, I was under the impression Mr Robson was the owner of the flat. There's clearly been some misunderstanding. I must say that you are most fortunate to be in possession of such a delightful property.'

Although Isabella felt resentful of the agent turning up without notice and assuming her flat belonged to Douglas, she was interested in hearing what its value was.

She smiled and the estate agent relaxed his shoulders. 'Let me show you around, Mr Wright.'

The estate agent left half an hour later, and Isabella sank back into her chair with a cigarette. 'This place is worth even more than Douglas thought it would be. Isn't it wonderful, Annie?'

'Chelsea is a popular place to live. Did Mr Robson tell you he'd spoken with an estate agent?'

'No, and it was rather cheeky of him to do so without telling me. I think he was also quite willing to create the impression he owned it too! I shall have to have a word with him about it.'

'I hope you don't think I'm speaking out of turn, Miss Trigwell, but I think it's impolite of him to take such an interest in your property.'

'I don't think you are speaking out of turn, Annie. I agree with you.'

'I think you need to be careful.'

'Oh, you know me, Annie, I'm very good at being careful.'

'I like Mr Robson, but I also know that money can do strange things to people. It can twist the mind.'

Isabella smiled. 'Thank you for being so concerned, Annie. Let's make sure we're both cautious.'

Chapter 35

'THIS MORNING HAS GONE WELL,' said Fred when Augusta returned to the bookshop. 'The Irish lady bought another Brontë book and the elderly gentleman bought another collection of poetry. It seems he wasn't frightened away by Lady Hereford's ghost story the other day.'

'Well that's good news.'

'In fact, he asked where she was today.'

Augusta laughed. 'Maybe we could employ her to entertain our customers?'

Fred asked how the investigation into Robert Trigwell's murder was progressing and Augusta told him. 'We're going to see Douglas Robson this evening. It seems he's very keen to marry Isabella Trigwell now that she's inherited a fortune.'

The sound of laughter from upstairs interrupted them.

'What on earth is that?' said Augusta. She watched in disbelief as two men, chatting animatedly, descended the stairs and headed for the door.

'Excuse me!' she called out. But they didn't hear. She marched after them and followed them out of the door.

They were so absorbed in their conversation, that she had to tap one of them on the shoulder.

He spun round. 'I beg your pardon?'

'What are you doing walking through my shop?'

'It's your shop?'

'Yes. I spoke to your colleague recently and asked him to stop using my shop as a shortcut to and from his office. He agreed. So why are you walking through my shop?'

'Which colleague?'

'I didn't ask his name. Dark hair. A thin moustache.'

'That would be Rogers.'

'He didn't tell you not to walk through my shop?'

'No.'

Augusta gritted her teeth. 'I'm going to have to speak to Mr Fitzwilliam or Mr Harper about this. You can't just walk through my shop whenever it pleases you! It's disruptive and unnerves my customers.'

'It's quicker.'

'So I understand.'

Augusta turned to the door of Fitzwilliam and Harper and pressed the doorbell.

'What are you doing?'

'Speaking to your managers.'

'We didn't mean anything by it. We didn't know we weren't supposed to use the door. It was Rogers's office, you see, but he was moved out and we've just moved in. He's been promoted and is now next to Fitzwilliam.'

'I'm not interested in your explanations any longer. I want to speak to your managers.'

Mr Fitzwilliam was a bald man with sleepy eyes and a quiet voice. He sat at his desk and examined his pen as

Augusta told him about his staff members using her shop for access.

'I'm very sorry they're disturbing your work,' he said. 'I shall ask my staff not to use that door in future.'

'But will they listen?' she asked, unconvinced that the staff would obey this languid man.

'Yes, I think so.' He turned his pen over in his hand and examined it from a different angle. He seemed to be humouring her with platitudes and merely waiting for her to leave his office.

'You *think* so Mr Fitzwilliam? Can I stress, please, the importance of you instructing your staff not to walk through my shop? It alarms my customers, and it's disruptive.'

'I understand you, Mrs Peel.'

She wanted to grab him by the shoulders and shake him awake.

'How would you like it if I walked through your offices, Mr Fitzwilliam?'

'Presumably you must have done so to find me here.'

Augusta sighed. There seemed little she could do or say to emphasise her request.

'If another member of your staff walks through my shop again, then I shall have to make a complaint to the landlord.'

'Sir Pritchard?'

'Yes.'

'He's a good friend of mine.'

Augusta felt her heart sink. It was going to be her word against Mr Fitzwilliam's.

Chapter 36

THAT EVENING, Augusta, Philip and Detective Sergeant Joyce stood in the hallway of Douglas Robson's Willesden home. His wavy-haired wife held a young child on her hip and eyed them suspiciously.

'What do you want?' she asked.

'A quick word with your husband please, Mrs Robson,' said Philip.

'What about?'

'Oh, hello!' came a voice from behind her. 'Goodness. What a crowd! How can I help, gentlemen? And lady?'

He wore a smart linen suit and had floppy, greying hair. He grinned broadly but Augusta noticed his smile didn't reach his eyes.

'We would like to know your whereabouts on Thursday the twenty-fourth of February,' said Philip.

His grin broke into a laugh. 'Well, that sounds very specific. May I ask why?'

'I would like you to answer my question first.'

'Very well.' He turned to his wife. 'I need to speak to

these people in the front room, Diana. Can you make sure the children stay out?'

'Yes.' She gave everyone a parting glare as Mr Robson ushered them into the front room. It was smaller and more simply furnished than Isabella Trigwell's flat. Augusta could understand why she and her money appealed to him.

'Can I get an idea of what this is all about?' he hissed as they sat themselves on the sofa and armchairs.

'I suspect you already have an idea, Mr Robson,' said Philip.

'Oh I do, do I? That's rather presumptuous of you, Detective Inspector.'

'The sooner you answer my questions, Mr Robson, the sooner we'll be finished and then you can get back to your family.'

He sighed, then pulled a pocket diary from his jacket and leafed through it. 'The twenty-fourth of February, you say? I don't appear to have done anything that evening.'

'You don't remember?'

'I thought for a moment it might have been the evening when I was at the Rotary Club dinner but that was the following evening.'

'You say you were doing nothing, so where were you?'

'Here.'

'You recall you were definitely here on that evening?'

'Yes.'

'At what time?'

'Well, that all depends on what time you're interested in, Detective Inspector. But I was here all evening.'

'Your wife will vouch for that?'

He scratched his nose. 'Of course. Now when are you going to tell me what all this is about?'

'What's the nature of your relationship with Miss Isabella Trigwell?'

He scowled and glanced at the door. 'I'd ask you not to discuss her while under my roof.'

'Can I infer from your reply that your relationship with her is unknown to your wife?'

He got to his feet. 'Yes,' he hissed. 'And you've no business coming to my home and mentioning it!'

'We're investigating the murder of Robert Trigwell. We need to gather all the information we can.'

'Isabella's extremely disappointed you haven't caught the killer yet.'

'I'm sure she is. We're doing our best, Mr Robson. And our job is made easier when everyone we speak to cooperates fully with the investigation.'

'Well, I've got nothing to tell you. I barely knew Robert. He kept himself to himself.'

'Isabella benefits substantially from his death.'

Mr Robson gave a dry laugh. 'What a thing to say about a grief-stricken lady.'

'You know what I'm referring to, Mr Robson. After the death of Mrs Trigwell, her son, Robert, inherited a sizeable fortune. Now that he has died, the estate passes to Isabella.'

'And it means nothing to her! She's just lost two members of her family. Have you any idea how much she's suffering?'

'Yes, I have some idea, Mr Robson. But it's important we can gather as much information as possible to find the person who attacked her brother. Miss Trigwell is a wealthy young woman now, can I ask what your plans for the relationship are?'

'No you may not. That's entirely the business of Miss Trigwell and myself.'

'You do realise that any attempts to hide information from the police could raise suspicion against you?'

'I'm not trying to hide anything from the police, I have my family to think about. This is all a rather delicate matter as you can appreciate, Detective Inspector, and it's one which I have great difficulty discussing under the roof of my family home.'

'Do you plan to leave your wife, Mr Robson?'

'No.'

'That's not what Miss Trigwell thinks. She told us you're planning to get married.'

He scratched the side of his face. 'Like I say, this is a delicate matter. And it's been difficult to discuss these things properly when she's been grieving for her mother and her brother.'

'If you were to divorce your wife and marry Miss Trigwell, then you could share her fortune,' said Augusta.

'Something which I have no interest in doing!'

'Does Miss Trigwell know you have no plans to divorce?'

'Not yet.' He sighed and sat down again. 'I've been planning to break the news to her, but it's not been easy because she's been so upset about everything. I would be lying if I said we have never discussed marriage. But I've decided it wouldn't be suitable and that I should, instead, put my efforts into my marriage.' His shoulders slumped, and he adopted a sorrowful expression. 'It's been a difficult few years. No marriage is perfect, and I found myself drifting apart from my wife. I met Isabella and she's a beautiful and charming lady, as you know. We have a firm friendship and I realise she would like to marry me.'

'So you don't plan to divorce your wife and marry your wealthy mistress?' asked Philip.

'No. And Isabella is not a mistress of mine, please don't describe her as that. She's a close friend, and that is all.'

'So close that you attend the meetings with her family

solicitor and take a keen interest in the value of the Trigwell estate?'

'Only because I want to make sure she doesn't get the wool pulled over her eyes. I'm sure the family solicitor is a decent chap, but one can never be too sure. Everything is complicated by the fact Robert didn't leave a will. There's a lot of work to be done and professionals can run rings around grieving ladies. They overcharge and don't always make the best decisions for their clients. They need to be kept in check. I don't want Isabella taken advantage of, so I'm helping to ensure she gets everything she's entitled to.'

'How noble of you, Mr Robson.'

'I like to think so. Isabella needs a lot of help at the moment. And although she misses her mother, she didn't enjoy living with her.'

'Is that so?'

'She was a very difficult woman. She didn't like me at all.'

'Why not?'

'I don't know! After all, I think most people find me a likeable fellow. Mrs Trigwell was just an odd lady. Isabella told me she never recovered from the death of Isabella's father so I suppose that had something to do with it.'

'Did Miss Trigwell's father like you?' asked Detective Sergeant Joyce.

'I never met him,' said Mr Robson.

Philip glared at Joyce to warn him off asking any more questions. Then he turned back to Mr Robson. 'Did you know Robert Trigwell was a regular visitor to Westminster Abbey?'

'No. I knew very little about him.'

'Have you heard of Aphra Behn?'

'No. Who's he?'

'She. A seventeenth-century writer.'

'Never heard of her. Why are you asking me these questions?'

'May we speak with your wife now?'

'My wife?' He paled. 'What can you possibly want to speak to her about?'

'Don't worry. We won't mention Miss Trigwell.'

'You'd better not!'

Chapter 37

Diana Robson perched on the edge of the armchair and pulled at a handkerchief. Beyond the closed door came the sound of her husband trying to placate a crying child.

'We'll make this as quick as possible, Mrs Robson,' said Philip. 'Can you tell us what your husband was doing on the evening of the twenty-fourth of February?'

'He's in trouble, isn't he? What has he done?'

'I'm not aware of him having done anything, but we're just carrying out some checks.'

'That's the night the man was attacked in Westminster Abbey, isn't it? I've read all the newspaper stories about it. Do you think Douglas did it?'

'No,' said Philip. Augusta knew this lie was designed to keep Mrs Robson calm. 'But we are checking on the whereabouts of many people that evening.'

'But my husband didn't even know the man who was attacked.'

'That may be so. But we're also looking for witnesses.'

'He didn't witness anything. He would have said.'

'Let's return to my original question, Mrs Robson. Can

you tell me where your husband was on the evening of the twenty-fourth of February?'

She gave this some thought. 'I don't think he was at home. He had a dinner somewhere.'

'The Rotary Club dinner?'

'No, I think that was the following evening. I remember reading about the murder in the newspaper the following morning and we talked about how shocked we both were. He had definitely been out that evening. I forget exactly where. He's been so busy with work recently that he's hardly been at home.'

Augusta felt sorry for Mrs Robson. She wished she could tell her what her cheating husband had been getting up to. Instead, she had to bite her lip. The troubles in the Robson marriage were no business of hers. She could only hope that Mrs Robson would find out soon.

'So you think your husband was out on the evening of the twenty-fourth of February?'

'Yes. I'm sure of it. But why don't you ask him?'

'We have,' said Philip. 'I just wanted to make sure your account tallied with his.'

'And does it?'

'The things people tell us must remain confidential, Mrs Robson.'

'Why can't you tell me what my husband told you?'

'I'm not obliged to share with you what he told us. Although you're quite entitled to ask him yourself.'

'Very well.'

Augusta imagined that would be an interesting conversation.

. . .

'So what do you think, Joyce?' Philip asked once they had they left the Robson household. 'Was Douglas Robson telling us the truth?'

'Yes, I think so,' said Joyce. 'He seems an honest man.'

'Even though he's cheating on his wife?'

'He said himself no marriage is perfect. And even if he's an adulterer, that doesn't mean he's a murderer.'

'True,' said Philip. 'We encounter a lot of dubious characters in this line of work and we have to be careful not to let our opinions of someone cloud our judgement.'

'Absolutely, sir.'

'But you need to pay more attention, Joyce, because it looks like Robson is lying. He said he was at home on the night of Robert Trigwell's murder but his wife said he was out.'

'Maybe his wife is lying?' said Joyce.

'I don't think she is. Don't you recall Mrs Hargreaves the housekeeper telling us Robson visited Miss Trigwell at eight o'clock that evening?'

'Oh yes, I remember now. I need to learn to notice these things.'

'I can't make my mind up if Robson is lying about the divorce,' said Augusta. 'He and Isabella have clearly got different opinions about it. I suspect that's because he's got himself into a pickle with his marriage.'

'It seems that way,' said Philip. 'You can imagine the scenario, can't you? The mistress is keen for him to leave his wife because she's tired of being the clandestine partner. He, however, is reluctant to turn his back on his marriage and leave the security of his wife, home and children.'

'So he tries to have the best of both worlds for as long as he possibly can.'

'That's about the measure of it. But does he have

designs on Miss Trigwell's money? From what he told us, he seems to have become involved with her while her mother was still alive. At that time, there seemed little chance of her inheriting the wealth she has now.'

'But perhaps he had a plan?' said Augusta.

'Such as what?'

'Do we know how Margaret Trigwell died?'

'No.'

'It would be interesting to find out if there were any suspicious circumstances.'

'You mean murder?' said Detective Sergeant Joyce.

'Yes,' said Augusta. 'What if Douglas Robson murdered Mrs Trigwell as well as Robert Trigwell?'

'Goodness,' said Philip. 'That's quite an accusation!'

'But not impossible.'

'You think Douglas Robson could be evil enough to befriend Isabella Trigwell and murder her family so he can access the family fortune?'

'Yes. I think he could be.'

Chapter 38

Augusta was repairing a copy of *Gulliver's Travels* when Philip and Detective Sergeant Joyce called at the bookshop the following afternoon. She didn't mind the interruption, but she was growing frustrated with the lack of time for book repairs.

'We've been making some investigations into Margaret Trigwell's death, haven't we, Joyce?' said Philip.

'That's right,' replied the young man. 'I obtained a copy of her death certificate from the Public Record Office on Chancery Lane. It stated the cause of her death was heart failure.' He gave a proud smile.

'So it can't have been murder,' said Augusta.

'Let's not leap to any assumptions yet,' said Philip. 'I telephoned the doctor who certified Mrs Trigwell's death. He told me the housekeeper, Annie Hargreaves, found Margaret Trigwell deceased in bed on the morning of the tenth of January. He attended and confirmed she died during the previous night.'

'Had she been unwell before she died?'

'A little. Apparently she'd been feeling under the

weather and he'd visited her a few days before she died. She had been suffering lethargy and a general malaise, apparently, but her death came as a surprise. The doctor says Miss Trigwell and her housekeeper were quite distressed. I asked him if there was any possibility her death could have been suspicious and he said there was not. He stood by his verdict of heart failure. One thing I've learned about doctors is they don't like having their diagnoses questioned.

'So I asked him to consider a hypothetical situation whereby a woman displaying signs of lethargy could be suffering the symptoms of poisoning. Eventually, he conceded it wasn't impossible because poisoning symptoms can be many and varied. But he was keen to remind me he felt Margaret Trigwell's death had been natural. The only way to be certain is to conduct a post-mortem. No post-mortem was carried out on Margaret Trigwell because her death wasn't deemed suspicious and a doctor had attended her shortly before she died. There is the possibility of exhumation, but we would need certain permissions for that.'

'Exhumation?' said Detective Sergeant Joyce. 'You mean dig her up again?'

'We prefer to use the phrase *exhumation*.'

'Ugh! You're not going to do that, are you?'

'Obviously no one wants to do that. But if there are questions over the cause of death, then it can be done. Many poisons can be detected in the body long after someone has died.'

'Ugh, what a job!'

Philip sighed. 'Joyce, please keep your schoolboy comments to yourself.'

'Schoolboy?'

'We're discussing a sensitive matter and maturity is

required. This job can provoke emotions at times, and it's important to remain professional.'

Joyce said nothing, seemingly wounded at being likened to a schoolboy.

'If there's a possibility Margaret Trigwell was poisoned, then we'll need to find out if Douglas Robson had access to her food and drink in the days before her death,' said Augusta. 'We need to speak to Miss Trigwell and her housekeeper again.'

Chapter 39

'OH, IT'S YOU LOT,' said Mrs Hargreaves when she answered the door. 'Can this please be quick? Miss Trigwell is exhausted by all these visits.'

'We'll be as quick as we can,' said Philip. Augusta followed him to the living room and Detective Sergeant Joyce tailed after.

'What is it now?' Isabella Trigwell sighed and placed her book about the French Riviera on the table beside her chair.

'We'd like to ask you about your mother,' said Philip, settling on the sofa.

'What does my mother have to do with anything?'

'I understand she died of heart failure.'

'Yes. But what about it?'

'We want to make sure her death wasn't suspicious.'

She sat forward, her eyes widening. 'Suspicious?'

'Your mother left a considerable fortune after she died, and we'd like to establish that nothing was done to hasten her death.'

'You think she was *murdered*?'

'I'm sure she wasn't, but we need to find out how she was during her last few days.'

Isabella pulled out a handkerchief. 'Oh, this is so upsetting!'

'I know. There's no easy way of discussing this, but we feel it needs to be done. Were you concerned about your mother in the days before she died?'

'A little. She wasn't very well. But I didn't think she would die!'

'What were her symptoms?'

'She felt weak, and she had headaches. She took to her bed. And then one morning...' Isabella began to sob. 'That's when Annie found her!'

'I'm sorry we're upsetting you, Miss Trigwell,' said Philip. 'I realise this isn't easy for you to talk about. May I ask who prepared your mother's food?'

She dabbed at her eyes. 'Annie. Why do you ask? Just a moment... Do you think she *poisoned* mother?'

'No, I'm sure a loyal housekeeper would have no desire to poison her employer. What about anyone else?'

'Prepared the food, you mean? No, just Annie.'

'Did you have anyone else to dine with you before your mother's death?' asked Augusta.

'Douglas.'

'What about your brother?'

'Yes, he dined with us a few times, too. Do you think he poisoned her? He would never have done such a thing!'

'We're just trying to build up a picture,' said Philip. 'May we speak with Mrs Hargreaves?'

'Of course.' Isabella called out. 'Annie!'

The housekeeper entered the room, wiping her hands on her apron.

'Thank you for joining us, Mrs Hargreaves,' said Philip. 'Miss Trigwell tells us you prepared all her mother's meals.'

'Yes. I cook everything here.'

'Was it possible someone else could have accessed Mrs Trigwell's food before she died?'

'I'm not sure what you mean.'

'While you were preparing the food, could a visitor have come into the kitchen and tampered with the food without you noticing?'

'Tampered?'

'Yes. By adding something. Poison, for example.'

'Poison?'

'That was just an example. Could it have happened?'

'No! You think someone poisoned Mrs Trigwell?'

'We don't know. The doctor said it was heart failure and I think that's the most likely explanation. We're just thinking about different possibilities.'

'We'd have known if she'd been poisoned.'

'I'm sure you would have.'

She put her hand on her chest as if trying to calm her breath.

'Please don't worry yourself about it, Mrs Hargreaves,' said Philip. 'I have to ask a lot of people questions. And sometimes they may seem strange questions.'

'Yes. I understand.'

'Please don't worry, Annie,' said Isabella. 'It's just a silly idea they've come up with. We know Mother wasn't poisoned. How about you make us some tea?'

Mrs Hargreaves smiled, clearly reassured by a comforting domestic task. 'Of course. It would be my pleasure, Isabella.'

'And please be careful not to put any poison in it.'

Mrs Hargreaves gave a small chuckle. 'Very well.'

Isabella waited until her housekeeper had left the room, then turned to Philip. 'She's easily upset, you know.'

'I can see that.'

'What do you mean by suggesting poisoning?'

'I'll be frank with you, Miss Trigwell. Did Douglas Robson have an opportunity to tamper with your mother's food or drink before she died?'

'No. You think Douglas poisoned my mother?'

'It's one of many theories we're considering.'

'Many theories? It sounds like you only have this one. You suspect him, don't you?'

'Do you know what Douglas Robson was doing on the evening of your brother's death?'

'I can't remember. Have you asked him?'

'He told us he was at home. His wife, however, told us he was out at a dinner.'

'Well, I'm sure you can appreciate he's had to tell his wife a few lies because of our affair.'

'But do you know where he was?'

'He came here about eight o'clock. I'm sure Annie told you that.'

'Do you know what he was doing before then?'

'He was busy at work. He works for Albemarle and Forester in the City, as you know. To get here for eight, he must have left there about half-past seven. To be entirely sure, you'll need to check with them. You've got this all wrong, you know. There's no chance my mother was poisoned. And Douglas is an innocent man. It's about time you caught my brother's murderer and stopped chasing your wild ideas!'

'So what do you think, Joyce?' asked Philip as they walked to Sloane Square tube station. 'Are we chasing wild ideas? Or are we on the right track?'

'I don't know.' Detective Sergeant Joyce shrugged.

Augusta noticed he had remained quiet throughout their visit to Miss Trigwell.

'What do you think, Augusta?' asked Philip.

'If Mrs Trigwell was poisoned, then the person with the best opportunity to do it was Annie Hargreaves.'

'Agreed. But it's difficult to understand why a house-keeper would poison her employer after working for her for a number of years.'

'There's also a possibility Mrs Trigwell's food or drink could have been interfered with at the dining table,' said Augusta. 'In which case, Miss Trigwell and Mr Robson could both be suspects.'

'And if we're looking for an opportunity Douglas Robson had to poison Mrs Trigwell, then that would be it,' said Philip. 'He would had to have done it without Miss Trigwell or her mother noticing, though. And perhaps Mrs Trigwell wasn't poisoned after all? Maybe we should listen to the doctor and accept his verdict of heart failure.'

'Perhaps we should,' said Augusta. 'But it needs further investigation. And we also need to find out exactly what Douglas Robson was doing at the time of Robert Trigwell's death.'

Chapter 40

AUGUSTA REFLECTED on the day as she tried to encourage Sparky to return to his cage for bedtime. He sat on his favourite spot on her curtain rail and regarded her with his head cocked to one side.

'Oh Sparky, this is all a fun game for you, isn't it?'

Lady Hereford had decreed that Sparky should roost in his cage between the hours of nine in the evening and seven in the morning. It was twenty-past nine now.

'It's past your bedtime,' Augusta said to him. But thoughts from the day were distracting her. Was it possible she and Philip were missing something obvious? Had they become too certain Douglas Robson was the murderer and were ignoring other possibilities?

She went over to her telephone, dialled the operator and asked to be put through to Philip's number on the Fulham exchange.

'Augusta!' said Philip. 'This is a nice surprise.'

'Is it?'

'Well, it's better than puzzling over my crossword. I'm getting nowhere with it. Lizard newts.'

'I'm sorry?'

'It's an anagram for a country, apparently. Anyway, what's prompted you to call?'

'I'm worrying that we've been thinking too much about Douglas Robson.'

'We should think about Alfred Smith again?'

'Yes. We're assuming Robert Trigwell died of the wounds he suffered in the attack at Westminster Abbey. But perhaps the wounds weren't fatal?'

'You think he could have survived them?'

'Possibly.'

'So they didn't look after him adequately in St Thomas's?'

'I'm sure they did. But there's a possibility someone at St Thomas's Hospital may not have wanted Robert to survive.'

'Alfred Smith.'

'Yes.'

'It was a surprise to discover he's training at the same hospital Trigwell was admitted to, wasn't it? Are you thinking Smith could have deliberately sabotaged his treatment?'

'It's a possibility.'

'And the motive?'

'Their relationship during the war threatened Smith's chances of marriage.'

'Yes, that's a strong motive. Mr Golding opposed the engagement because he knew about the close friendship between the two men. But did Smith know that Mr Golding had made the enquiries?'

'Perhaps Mr Golding told him what he'd heard from the colonel?'

'Perhaps he did.'

'And Smith was so enraged that he murdered Trigwell.'

'For revenge? To silence him?'

'Either of those could apply. Possibly both.'

'In which case, you could argue that Smith was extremely lucky that the man he wished to murder happened to have been admitted to the hospital he was working in.'

'Perhaps he ordered the attack on Robert?'

'Now there's a thought. Or even carried out the attack himself. And when he was unsuccessful in murdering him immediately, he then finished him off as he lay in his hospital bed.'

'Not nice.'

'I don't know about this theory, Augusta. It would mean Alfred Smith is an extremely cunning man indeed.'

'Perhaps he is. I think we need to establish when Mr Golding told Smith he didn't want him to marry his daughter. If it happened before Trigwell's murder, then there could be something in it. We need to ask Smith where he was when Trigwell was murdered.'

'And we need to find out if Smith was seen on or near the ward where Trigwell was admitted. And perhaps that's why Trigwell mentioned the name Alfred Smith. Not because he wanted to find him, but because he was the person harming him in the hospital. But why did he mention his regimental number?'

'Alfred Smith is a common name. Perhaps it was to ensure we found the right one,' said Augusta.

'Let's go to St Thomas's hospital tomorrow and have another word with him.'

'And there's Simon Granger too.'

'The evasive work colleague at the funeral? He's a good suggestion. We've not looked into him at all yet, have we? Let's visit the J Baker offices as well. I'll try and get away before Joyce latches onto me. I don't want to spend the day babysitting him again. I'll see you in the morning.'

'Switzerland.'

'I beg your pardon?'

'The lizard newts anagram.'

'How did I not see that? Thank you, Augusta.'

Chapter 41

ALFRED SMITH SAT glum-faced in the room overlooking the Thames at St Thomas's Medical School. He wasn't pleased to see Augusta and Philip and kept glancing out of the window to where low clouds scurried over the river and Westminster.

'We'd like to establish when you spoke to Mr Golding about marrying his daughter,' said Philip.

'It was the twenty-first of February.'

Augusta recalled that Robert Trigwell was attacked three days later, on the twenty-fourth.

'Thank you for the swift and accurate reply,' said Philip. 'Usually when we ask such questions, people spend ages leafing through a diary and telling us they can't remember anything. How did you feel after your conversation with him?'

Alfred's jaw clenched. 'Anger,' he said. 'And embarrassment. I went straight home. I didn't feel welcome in the house anymore.'

'Why do you think Mr Golding refused to give the engagement his blessing?' asked Augusta.

'I don't know. You'd have to ask him.'

'Is it possible he knew about your friendship with Robert Trigwell?'

'I can't see how.'

'We've spoken to Captain Lowther at the East Surrey Regiment. He was your platoon commander for a while, is that right?' said Philip.

'Captain Lowther? How is he?'

'He seems well.'

'Good.'

'He asked after you and we told him you're training to be a doctor here at St Thomas's. He seemed pleased to hear it. He also told us he received an enquiry about you from a mutual friend of a man whose daughter you wished to marry.'

Alfred paled. 'The enquiry came from Mr Golding?'

'We think it must have done. Captain Lowther didn't know the name of the man making enquiries. A retired colonel contacted him and he believes the colonel was a member of the same gentleman's club as Mr Golding.'

Alfred gave a long sigh and stared up at the ceiling.

'Are you alright, Mr Smith?' asked Augusta.

Eventually, he lowered his head. His eyes were damp. 'Yes, I think so. Well... I suppose I'm not really. No matter how hard you try, you can never escape your past, can you?'

'It can have a habit of catching up with you,' said Philip.

'Yes, it can. I suppose I should explain a few things. There were rumours about my friendship with Robert, but they were just rumours. And when such accusations are levelled against you, any attempt to defend yourself is dismissed. There's nothing you can do. I can only imagine Captain Lowther told both you and the retired colonel about those rumours. In which case, I think it's quite obvious why Mr Golding is unhappy about an engagement between me and his daughter. I've never been found guilty of any wrongdoing, and yet people have made their minds up about me. Mud has a habit of sticking.'

'But did you know Mr Golding had made these enquiries before Mr Trigwell's death?'

Alfred met Philip's eye. 'No, I didn't.'

'Why did you tell people at Robert Trigwell's funeral that your name was James Godwin?'

'My identity was none of their business.'

'But why the secrecy? You didn't tell Miss Golding that you knew Roger Trigwell, despite his murder having filled many column inches in the newspapers.'

'I'm a private person, Detective Inspector. What more can I say? I realise that being a private person isn't helpful when police officers are after information. At the very worst, I suppose it looks like I'm protecting my guilt. But I've learned, over the years, that it suits me to say as little about myself as possible.'

'Did you know Robert Trigwell was admitted here in St Thomas's hospital?' asked Augusta.

'Not at the time. I only read that he died here in the newspaper reports.'

'Did you think it was a coincidence that you were training at the same hospital Robert died in?'

'It's surprising. But not a coincidence. This is a large hospital and admits a lot of patients. I suppose there are bound to be people I've met in the past being treated here.'

'Would you have visited Robert if you had known he was here?' asked Philip.

Alfred took some time to answer this. 'I think I would have liked to,' he said eventually. 'But I think I would have been too worried to do so, given the rumours people had spread about us. And I think my appearance at his bedside might have caused him some distress.'

'Why?'

'Just because we hadn't seen each other in so long and… it wouldn't have been the right thing to do.'

'And your friendship with him sparked rumours which led to Mr Golding's hostility towards you.'

'I suppose it did.'

'Are you sure you didn't know he was trying to contact you?' asked Augusta.

'Quite sure.' He frowned.

'Perhaps he sent you letters which you destroyed?'

'No, I didn't receive any letters.'

'A telephone call, perhaps?'

'No.'

'Perhaps if he had made contact, you would have been reminded of the rumours,' said Philip. 'They could have threatened your chances of marriage. Perhaps they could have threatened your profession too?'

'That's the ridiculous nature of it!' he snapped, his face reddening.

'Perhaps it suits you that Mr Trigwell is no longer around?'

'Suits me? Not at all. It makes no difference to me. Are you suggesting I had a hand in his death? That's impossible!'

'We need to establish where you were on the night of Thursday, the twenty-fourth of February.'

'I was in my room here in the medical school.'

'Can anyone vouch for that?'

'I can't believe you're asking me this, Detective Inspector!'

'I realise this isn't easy, Mr Smith. It's something we

have to check with everyone we speak to. Can someone provide you with an alibi for the twenty-fourth?'

'I finished my studies for the day at five and dined at eight o'clock. People would have seen me around, but I can't think of anyone specifically.'

'Did you visit Mr Trigwell when he was here?'

'No.'

'Not even during the night when you were less likely to be spotted?'

'Any visitor to the ward at that time would have been quite obvious.'

'I see.'

'What are you suggesting? That I harmed him while he was here?' He leant forward and jabbed his forefinger into the table. 'Let me make myself quite clear, I didn't wish to resume any form of friendship with Robert Trigwell. Doing so would have resurrected many troublesome memories from the past. Despite that, I didn't wish him dead. I feel that both of us deserved a chance at life, just like every man who fought. We had the privilege of returning when many others didn't. God spared us both, and he didn't deserve what happened to him.'

'No, he didn't,' said Philip. 'One more question, if I may. What's the status of your engagement to Sylvia Golding now?'

'I don't see why it's your business, but she's thinking about what to do.'

'So you're engaged? Or not engaged?'

Alfred sat back in his chair and gave Philip a cold glance. 'I actually don't know.'

Chapter 42

AUGUSTA AND PHILIP travelled by taxi from St Thomas's Hospital to the offices of J Baker in Gerrard Street, Soho.

'So what are your thoughts on Alfred Smith now?' asked Philip.

'I think he could be a murderer,' said Augusta. 'Do you?'

'I can see how he would have felt driven to it. It could have been a case of desperation. A yearning for a respectable life. But if he murdered Robert Trigwell, then we need to work out when. Did he attack him in the abbey cloisters? Or as he lay injured in a hospital bed?'

The taxi pulled up in Soho, opposite a shop with colourful spring fashions in the window.

'This is where it all started,' said Philip with a smile as they climbed out of the car.

'What did?'

'When we began working together again last year. Flo's Club is just up there, see it?'

'Of course! I'd forgotten it was on Gerrard Street.'

'Poor Jean Taylor lost her life here. You got caught up in it, then pulled my name into it.'

'Sorry about that.'

'I'm glad you did.'

'Are you?'

'Yes. Because it's been good working with you again, Augusta. And it's been more enjoyable than wartime Belgium, that's for sure.'

They exchanged a smile before stepping into the offices of J Baker.

'You wish to speak to Simon Granger?' asked the lady behind the reception desk. She had bobbed copper hair and thin pencilled eyebrows.

'Yes please,' said Philip.

'Please excuse me a moment while I speak to Mr Baker.'

Augusta and Philip waited as the receptionist left her desk.

'*The* Mr Baker?' Augusta whispered to Philip. 'The same Baker as J Baker?'

'Could be. Or maybe the son of the founder? There seems to be a problem with us being able to speak to Mr Granger. I wonder what's going on?'

A few moments later, they were shown into Mr Baker's spacious office. Photographs of branches of Baker's Tea Rooms adorned the walls. Augusta recognised some of the central London ones.

Mr Baker had white hair, white whiskers and half-moon spectacles.

'Do take a seat,' he said, gesturing at two chairs. 'You're colleagues of Sergeant Hamilton?'

'No,' said Philip. 'I'm Detective Inspector Fisher of Scotland Yard and this is my colleague, Mrs Peel.'

'Also from the Yard?'

'No, I'm an independent investigator.'

'I see. And what about Hamilton?'

'I'm afraid I don't know who you mean,' said Philip.

'He's the one I've been dealing with. At Vine Street police station.'

'Regarding what?'

'Granger, of course. That's why you're here, isn't it?'

'Yes. Is Granger in trouble?'

'You should know. You're the police!'

Philip cleared his throat and Augusta could tell he was mustering some patience. 'It sounds like you and Mr Granger have been dealing with C Division. As a detective at Scotland Yard, I'm not aware of all the investigations being carried out by the various divisions. Perhaps you could tell me what you've been speaking to Sergeant Hamilton about?'

'Granger.'

'And what's he done?'

'He's been committing fraud. Surely that's why you want to speak to him?'

'We came here to speak to him about something else, but please tell us more.'

'It appears he's been stealing money from the company for some time now. Right beneath our noses! I called the police in and they've been busy going through the books and speaking to my staff. So you can see, Detective Inspector, just how trying the circumstances currently are.'

'I'm very sorry to hear it, Mr Baker.'

'I trusted him a great deal.'

'I expect you did.'

'And he took me for a fool.'

'But he's been caught now.'

'He certainly has!'

'We spoke briefly with Mr Granger at Robert Trigwell's funeral. He didn't want to say a great deal to us. Did he and Mr Trigwell work together?'

'They did. Mr Trigwell was a senior clerk who reported to Mr Granger. Shortly before his death, Mr Trigwell told me he'd found some anomalies in the accounts. He couldn't be sure if they were mistakes or deliberate, but he suspected a junior clerk called Harry Lewis was responsible.'

'When was this?'

'Three or four weeks ago. Not long before he died. We've now discovered that Granger was behind it all.' He sighed. 'You could have knocked me down with a feather. Always liked the chap. Always trusted him. And all along he was taking me for a fool.'

'You have my sympathy, Mr Baker. What an awful time for you.'

'At least you lot are looking into him now. And I want every penny he stole from me recovered.'

'Absolutely Mr Baker. I think we need to pay a visit to Sergeant Hamilton at Vine Street.'

Vine Street police station was a ten-minute walk from Gerrard Street.

'Simon Granger is proving to be interesting indeed,' said Philip as they walked along Shaftesbury Avenue. The street was famous for its theatres and the shows were advertised on big colourful hoardings. 'It seems Robert Trigwell discovered a fraud was being committed and then he died shortly afterwards. Could Simon Granger have been his killer?'

'He could well have been.'

'Douglas Robson, Alfred Smith and now Simon Granger,' said Philip. 'Hopefully we can charge one of them with Trigwell's murder very soon.'

Sergeant Hamilton was a curly-haired man with a broken tooth. In a police station meeting room, he showed Philip and Augusta the thick file he had prepared on Simon Granger.

'We've ascertained that Granger instructed a junior clerk, Harry Lewis, to make entries into the ledger which were fictitious. Paper records appear to have been created to explain the fictitious entries. We believe the paper records are also fictitious. Granger's intention was to use the fictitious records to account for money he was withdrawing for his own personal use.'

'And what does Mr Granger say about all this?'

'He denies it, of course. But we've gathered a lot of evidence and he hasn't really got a leg to stand on.'

'I know the feeling.'

Sergeant Hamilton glanced at Philip's walking stick which was leaning against the table. 'Oh, I'm sorry, sir, for my comment. I shouldn't have—'

Philip laughed. 'There's no need to apologise, I thought it was amusing. It looks like you're doing some excellent work here, Sergeant Hamilton.'

'Thank you, sir.'

'Has Simon Granger mentioned Robert Trigwell to you?'

'No, sir.'

'Apparently, Trigwell came across this fraud a few weeks ago. I'd like to speak to Granger about him.'

'I have plans to interview Granger tomorrow, sir. You're more than welcome to join us.'

'Thank you, Sergeant. I shall.'

Chapter 43

Simon Granger sat in the interview room with his arms folded. He was bigger and broader than both the men sitting opposite him. If he wasn't in a police station, then he would knock the pair of them out with no problem at all. The older one would be easy because he used a walking stick. The younger, curly-haired one would probably put up more of a fight, but his broken tooth suggested he had already been punched in the mouth recently. If they were in the King's Head pub now, he would have already knocked the pair of them out and be walking out of the door.

And where was Lewis in all of this? He was the man who had got him into this mess and there was no sign of him being hauled in front of the detectives. He was another one who had to watch out.

The detective and the sergeant had a thick file of paper in front of them. The police liked to leaf through papers during interviews to create the impression they had collected lots of information. Most of the papers probably had nothing on them. He could see where all this was going. He felt the need to take charge.

'I know what you're going to do,' said Simon. 'You're going to fire all sorts of questions at me and most of them will be irrelevant. To save everyone's time, how about I tell you exactly what happened? Then we won't have a long, drawn-out conversation which is going to waste your time more than mine.'

'Very well,' said the Scotland Yard detective, resting back in his chair. 'I like a man willing to cooperate and make things easy for us. Let's hear your explanation.'

Simon hadn't expected it to be quite so easy. He cleared his throat and began. 'Well, to begin with, you've got the wrong man sitting in front of you.'

'Have we? That seems rather remiss of us. Who's the right man?' asked the detective.

'Harry Lewis.'

'And who's he?'

'A junior clerk. He may be junior, but don't let that fool you. The boy's clever. Even I'm willing to admit that. Now, for some time, I've been concerned about the departmental accounts. There were a few things which weren't adding up. Literally and figuratively.' He thought this phrase made him sound intelligent, so he paused a little to let it sink in before continuing. 'I went over the numbers again and again and realised there were some entries which seemed spurious.' Another intelligent word. He was enjoying this. 'I like to be diligent about things, so I attempted to track down the paperwork associated with these entries. It took some searching, and I eventually found it in a folder at the back of the filing cabinet. The sort of place you'd expect someone to put something they don't want other people to find.'

He knew, because he had put it there himself.

'The paperwork appeared to be in order, but there was something about it which didn't seem right. It was a bit too perfect and pristine. I'll tell you what I mean by that. Usually, the papers in our files have reached the office via the postal system. I'm sure you're aware how dog-eared some envelopes are by the time the postman has finally delivered them. Knocked and battered about. Once they arrive in the office and are opened, they usually spend some time on someone's desk. They may be clipped and stapled and generally roughed about a bit more. Perhaps a stray drop of tea or flick of cigarette ash finds its way onto the documentation too. Anyway, suffice it to say that, by the time the papers are filed away, some of them have been subjected to the rigours of daily existence. Now, if you were to open one of our files, you would discover at least some papers in there to be a little worn or distressed in some way. Not so in the file I found. All the papers were perfect, as if someone had merely typed the necessary information onto them and filed them into the folder immediately. What's more, each seemed to have been typed on the same machine and on the same type of paper. There was too much similarity between them. In fact, you're free to examine them yourselves.'

'I have the file,' said Sergeant Hamilton. 'And your observation on the condition of the papers is correct. There's little doubt they're forgeries.'

'So it seems we're all agreed on that,' said Detective Inspector Fisher. 'The question is, did you know about those papers?'

'No. I had no idea what Harry Lewis was up to. Why would I?'

'You didn't instruct him to create the paperwork for each fraudulent entry?'

'No.'

'Whether you knew about the fraud or not is the concern of Sergeant Hamilton,' said the Scotland Yard detective. 'What I'm concerned with is Robert Trigwell's involvement in all of this.'

'He may have been involved, I couldn't say. Lewis will tell you if he decides to come clean about his heinous actions.'

'We believe Robert Trigwell discovered the fraudulent entries. Did he speak to you about them?'

Simon took a breath. He had to be careful about what he said. Robert Trigwell was dead, and he knew the Scotland Yard detective was looking for a motive behind his murder.

'Yes, he spoke to me about it.'

'And what did you discuss?'

'The errors Trigwell had spotted.'

'You didn't know about them until Mr Trigwell mentioned them?'

'No. I had no idea what Lewis was up to.'

'How did you know it was Lewis?'

'Because he was responsible for that side of things.'

'Even though your signature was on some of the documents?'

'Lewis forged it. I should think that much was obvious.'

'And as far as Robert Trigwell was concerned, you were grateful to him for spotting the errors?'

'Absolutely.'

'Did you tell him that?'

'I'm not sure that I did at the time because I was so shocked about what had been uncovered. I'm worried actually that I was a little sharp with Trigwell. Purely out of anger, of course. They warn against shooting the messenger, but I'm afraid we're all a little guilty of lashing out when we hear something we don't want to. So I was gruff with him. I'm not afraid to be honest about that. I was planning to find a moment to apologise to him. But that moment obviously never came. A week or two later, he was dead.'

Chapter 44

AUGUSTA RECEIVED a telephone call from Philip that evening.

'How was the interview with Simon Granger?' she asked.

'If you're asking if I think he could have murdered Robert Trigwell, then the answer is yes.'

'Really?'

'He's an obnoxious gentleman and thinks he's far cleverer than he actually is. Take my advice Augusta and stay out of his way.'

'Alright then.'

'I mean it.'

There was a serious tone in Philip's voice which worried her. 'Is everything alright?'

'No, it's not.'

'What's happened?'

'The commissioner has taken me off the case, Augusta.'

'No!' Her stomach plummeted. 'He can't do that!'

'I'm afraid he can.'

'But he's ruining the investigation. You've done so much work on this!'

'Which can apparently be handed over to someone else.'

'What reason did he give you?'

'I should step aside for another detective to gain some valuable experience.'

'Not…'

'Yes. Joyce.'

'But he's only just joined Scotland Yard! And he's the commissioner's son!'

'The powers that be clearly know what they're doing.'

'No, they don't!'

'I was being sarcastic, Augusta.'

'Of course. I'm sorry, I'm just so angry! Can't you refuse to be moved off the case?'

'No. I can only follow orders. I've been told off as well.'

'For what?'

'For calling Joyce a schoolboy.'

'But he *is* a schoolboy!'

'He tells tales like one, that's for sure.'

'But Philip, you can't be moved off the case. It will never be solved now.'

'It will if you continue to work on it, Augusta.'

'There's no chance whatsoever of me working with Joyce!'

'I don't blame you.'

She felt tears spring into her eyes. 'Well, that's it then! We won't get anywhere with it. And all our hard work will be for nothing.'

'It doesn't have to be. But I completely understand why you don't want to work with Joyce.'

'What are you going to work on instead?'

'Apparently my expertise is needed for a project on reorganising all of Scotland Yard's files.'

'I didn't know you had any expertise in that.'

'I don't. It's just an excuse to take me off the case, Augusta. We've done the hard work by narrowing it down to three suspects and now Joyce will get the glory.'

'He doesn't deserve it!'

'Few people ever do. You'll keep me posted, won't you?'

'On what?'

'On how it all goes.'

'I'm not working with Joyce.'

'I know you're not. But you'll do something, I know you will, Augusta. I've never known you walk away from a case before it's solved.'

She smiled and felt a tear roll down her cheek. 'You know me too well, Philip.'

Chapter 45

THE FOLLOWING MONDAY, Augusta stood on the breezy corner of Cheapside and Queen Victoria Street in the City of London. Bankers and stockbrokers dashed past her in smart dark suits, and traffic queued at the busy junction at the Bank of England.

Augusta walked a few steps down Cheapside and came across a sign for Albemarle and Forester. Douglas Robson's employer.

After the disappointing telephone conversation with Philip, Augusta had written a list of everything she needed to do. She planned to tackle the list in a calm, methodical manner. She wasn't going to allow her anger about Philip's treatment to get the better of her.

The first task on her list was to establish an alibi for Douglas Robson for the time Robert Trigwell was attacked. In the marbled foyer of Albemarle and Forester, she asked the bespectacled man at the reception desk if she could speak to Douglas Robson's manager.

'Douglas Robson? I'm afraid he left a while ago.'

'Really? That's a surprise. How long ago?'

'I think it must have been six months. Possibly longer.'

'My name is Mrs Peel. Does Mr Robson's manager still work here?'

'He does.'

'Please can I speak to him?'

The receptionist nodded and picked up a telephone receiver. After a brief conversation, he put the receiver down and turned back to Augusta. 'Mr Dingle will meet with you shortly.'

'Thank you.'

Mr Dingle was a short man with a round face and thinning hair. His shoes tapped on the marble floor. 'Mrs Peel? I understand you're enquiring about someone who used to work here. Douglas Robson?'

'That's right. I'd like to know how long ago it was when he left this company.'

'Let me think. What are we now? March? I think it must have been last June. Why do you ask?'

'Because I've met him and he claims to be still working here.'

He raised his eyebrows. 'Really? That's an odd thing for him to say.'

'Do you know if he went on to other employment after he left here?'

'As far as I'm aware, no.' He lowered his voice. 'He left under a bit of a cloud, you see, and I was unwilling to provide him with a reference. Between you and me, I'm not enormously surprised he didn't find employment elsewhere.'

'What was the cloud he left under?'

'He was generally quite poor at his job. Lazy. He was good at talking about work but not much good at getting it done. Have you seen him recently?'

'Yes. He's currently currying favour with a wealthy spinster.'

'That sounds like Robson. I can only imagine he hasn't found any further employment and has told you he's still working here so he can maintain some respectability.'

'I suspect that's exactly what he's doing. Thank you for your time, Mr Dingle.'

'No problem at all. It was a pleasure speaking with you, Mrs Peel. I hope you don't mind me asking, but what's your interest in Robson? Are you a friend?'

'No. I suppose you could call me an investigator.'

His eyebrows raised again. 'Really? Has he been up to something?'

'I don't know yet.'

'I'll happily tell you now that it doesn't surprise me. Tell that wealthy spinster to keep him away from her money.'

Chapter 46

'Douglas Robson has been lying about his job?' Fred fed a seed to Sparky. 'Presumably Isabella Trigwell doesn't know that.'

'No. I don't think anyone knows apart from me.' Augusta thought of his motor car and his family home in Willesden. 'I don't know how he's been able to get by with no income. He must be getting money from somewhere.'

'But where?'

'That's what I need to find out.'

The bell on the door sounded and a young man with fair hair and a sparse moustache stepped in.

Augusta gave a quiet groan.

'It's the detective who's replaced Philip?' whispered Fred.

'Yes.'

'Mrs Peel!' Detective Sergeant Joyce strode up to the counter with a spring in his step. 'How are you this afternoon?'

'Extremely disappointed that Detective Inspector

Fisher has been removed from the investigation into Robert Trigwell's murder.'

'I'm sorry to hear it. I have some news which will cheer you up, though.'

'Is that so?'

'Yes. It's something which the commissioner of Scotland Yard, Sir Graham Joyce, has personally requested. He happens to be my father, by the way.'

Augusta said nothing, so he cleared his throat and continued. 'As you probably know, it's been the custom in recent years for Scotland Yard to employ the services of lady detectives. It's finally been recognised that women can be just as clever at solving crimes as men!' He followed this with a grin which Augusta refused to return.

'I'm a bookseller,' she said. 'Not a lady detective.'

'Well, what I'm presenting to you today is an exciting opportunity. The commissioner is offering to pay you a generous sum in return for your continued assistance with the Trigwell murder case. If he's happy with your work, then there's the possibility of being paid for your assistance with further cases, too. As I understand it, you've not received any payment for your services to date?'

'No. Detective Inspector Fisher offered me payment when he asked for my assistance with the Soho murder, but I refused.'

'Well, I'm pleased to offer you the possibility of an ongoing paid opportunity.' He held out a hand for her to shake.

She didn't move. 'No, thank you.'

His face fell. 'I'm sorry?'

'I don't want an ongoing paid opportunity. I'm a bookseller.'

'But you've been assisting Detective Inspector Fisher.'

'Because he's an old friend.'

'You now have the chance to have a formal arrangement with Scotland Yard. A *paid* arrangement.'

'It's not what I want.'

'I see.' Detective Sergeant Joyce scratched at his temple. 'I suppose there's been some sort of misunderstanding, then.'

'Not really. Neither you nor your father have asked me what I want.'

'And what do you want?'

'I want Detective Inspector Fisher to be working on the Trigwell case again.'

'I'm afraid that's not possible. He's been moved to work on something else.'

'Then I shall move on to something else, too.'

'Do you realise what you're turning down, Mrs Peel?'

'Yes.'

'I see. I must say that your help really would be appreciated on this case. You've been helping with it from the very start.'

'You don't need to be reliant on my help, Detective Sergeant, especially when Detective Inspector Fisher is more than competent enough to be in charge.'

'So you're turning me down?'

'Yes I am. I wish you luck with it.'

Augusta watched him leave.

'I admire your stubbornness, Mrs Peel,' said Fred, once the young detective was outside on the street.

Augusta smiled. 'Is stubbornness a quality to admire?'

'Sometimes. Are you really going to stop working on the case, though? You've done so much, it would be a shame to stop now.'

'I have no intention of stopping, Fred. Just don't tell Detective Sergeant Joyce.'

Chapter 47

'HAVE you read the newspaper this morning, Mrs Peel?' asked Fred the following day.

'Not yet. What's that lorry doing outside the shop? It's blocking all the light.'

Then she startled at a sudden scraping noise. 'And what on earth is *that*?'

Augusta stepped out from behind the counter to see two men in overalls carrying a desk down the staircase. The legs of the desk knocked noisily against the bannisters.

'Careful!' she shouted. 'What are you doing?'

The two men stopped.

'We're just taking this desk out.'

'Through my shop? Why can't you use the other door?'

'This one's easier.'

'Not for me, it's not! Why are you moving a desk?'

'The bookkeepers are moving out.'

'But they've only just moved in!'

'Have they? Well, we wouldn't know about that. We were just asked to move the furniture out.'

'Well, can I ask that you take it out through the other door? You're disturbing my customers!'

'Alright. But given that we're already halfway down the stairs with this one, is it alright to carry on our way?'

'Yes,' she replied through clenched teeth. 'And then lock the door and don't come through it ever again!'

'Very well, madam. Apologies for the disturbance.'

'And mind the paintwork.'

'Yes, madam.'

She watched them intently as they carefully manoeuvred the desk around the newel post at the end of the staircase, then carried it through the shop.

'Shall I open the door for you?' she offered. She kept the tone of her voice cold so they wouldn't think she had forgiven them.

'Thank you, madam.'

'I'd like to help you get out as quickly as possible.'

She shut the door on them as soon as they were outside in the rain.

'How strange the bookkeepers are moving out already,' she said as she walked back to the counter.

'I think they all grew too terrified to walk through your shop,' said Fred.

'Good. With a bit of luck, I scared them off.'

'Have you read the newspaper this morning?'

'Not yet.'

'You'll want to see this,' said Fred, pointing at the headline. *Man Murdered in Royal Oak*. 'It says here his name was Douglas Robson.'

Chapter 48

'THE ARTICLE REPORTS that Robson left the King's Head pub in Royal Oak shortly after nine o'clock,' said Fred. 'He planned to drive to his home in Willesden. But he didn't go straight to his car. Instead, he went to the rear of the pub. Presumably the murderer enticed him there. The most logical explanation is that he knew his killer, I can't think how a complete stranger could have encouraged him to go round the back.'

'A woman?'

'It could have been couldn't it? The article says he was alone when he left the pub but it's possible someone could have approached him once he was outside. It's very similar to Mr Trigwell's death. A knife wound in his side.'

'It could be the same assailant,' said Augusta. 'Could you mind the shop for me while I visit Isabella Trigwell?'

Mrs Hargreaves looked tired and drawn when she answered the door. 'I never thought I'd say this, Mrs Peel, but I'm pleased to see you. It's nice to have a familiar face here. Miss Trigwell's in an awful state.'

'I'm not surprised.'

Augusta placed her wet umbrella in the umbrella stand and followed the housekeeper to the living room where Isabella Trigwell lay on a sofa. She was dressed in black, but she wore no make-up today. She looked washed out and older than her years.

'I'm sorry to hear about Douglas Robson,' Augusta said.

'Thank you,' said Isabella in a weak voice. 'Perhaps you'll believe me now when I tell you he was innocent.'

Augusta nodded.

'Where's the detective?'

'He's not working on your brother's case anymore.'

'But you are?'

'Unofficially. Officially, Detective Sergeant Joyce is in charge.'

'The young one?'

'Yes.'

Isabella sighed and stared at the wall. She looked like a woman who had given up on life.

'It's as if someone's punishing her,' said Mrs Hargreaves. 'Taking away everyone she cares about. I don't understand it.'

'When did you last see Douglas Robson?' Augusta asked Isabella.

'Yesterday. He came here after he'd finished work.'

Augusta hadn't the heart to tell her he had left his job long ago.

'He got here about seven o'clock,' continued Isabella. 'But he didn't stay long because he told me he'd arranged to meet friends for dinner.'

'In the King's Head?' A pub wasn't the usual meeting place for dinner.

'Maybe he went to dinner before he went to the pub? I don't know. He didn't tell me his exact plans.'

'How was he when you saw him yesterday?'

'He was fine. Nothing seemed to be bothering him and he hadn't had a disagreement with anyone that I was aware of. It's a mystery.'

'He was attacked in a similar manner to your brother,' said Augusta. 'I think it must be the same killer.'

'And what if they come for Isabella next?' said Mrs Hargreaves, her eyes wide with worry. 'What then?'

'We have to catch them before then.'

Chapter 49

Augusta flagged down a taxi outside Miss Trigwell's flat. The journey to Royal Oak took twenty minutes through rainy Belgravia, Hyde Park and Bayswater.

The King's Head was a large, shabby pub which stood at the junction of Harrow Road and a bridge over the railway lines. A young police constable loitered outside.

'I'm Augusta Peel,' she said to him. 'I'm assisting Detective Inspector Fisher of Scotland Yard.' This would have been true a few days previously, and she hoped he wouldn't question the small fib. 'Can you show me where Mr Robson was attacked?'

The constable nodded and led her down the side of the pub. A low wall separated the pub from a wide stretch of railway lines. Some served a nearby goods yard while the rest led to Paddington railway station close by. The wind blew the rain against Augusta and the constable as they stood on an unevenly paved area next to a coal store and some bins.

'The landlord found him here,' said the constable. 'It

was dark at the time. There's not a lot of lighting around here.'

A train rumbled past. 'Noisy, too.' Augusta had to raise her voice to make herself heard. 'Few people would have heard anything when he was attacked. Has the knife been found?'

'It was thrown onto the railway tracks.'

'Do you know what sort of knife it was?'

'Just an ordinary one.'

'Like a kitchen knife?'

'I suppose it could have been.'

Augusta sighed and glanced around again. It was a bleak location. Although she had disliked Douglas Robson, she couldn't help feeling some sympathy for him.

Inside the pub, the landlord had just opened for the day. He had a wide pugnacious face and his shirt sleeves were rolled up his thick arms. One forearm was tattooed with an anchor and the other had a heart with a dagger through it.

Augusta introduced herself. 'I'm an investigator and I've been working with Scotland Yard on a murder case.'

The landlord sighed. 'I spent most of yesterday evening talking to the police. And this morning too. I told them to clear off so I could get on with opening my pub. I would close it for the day out of respect for Douglas, but I know he wouldn't have wanted me to. His friends will be down soon, so we'll raise a toast for him then. I've told the police everything I know. What do you want?'

'I think Douglas's murder could be linked to another which I've been working on for a few weeks. Who was Douglas Robson with last night?'

'Well, I'll tell you what I've already told the coppers, although I don't see why I've got to keep repeating myself.

Robson was sat in that corner over there.' He pointed at a large, round table. 'He was with some friends. It was their usual spot.'

'Which friends?'

'The regulars. So last night we had Barnes, Granger, Leith and Morris.' He counted them off on his chubby fingers.

'Granger?'

'Yeah. What of him?'

'What's his first name?'

'Simon.'

Augusta's stomach gave an excitable flip. Robson and Granger must have known each other. 'I might know him,' she said. 'Do you know what he does for a living?'

'Blimey, you ask a lot of questions, don't you? He was working at… oh, what's the place called?' He scratched his head.

'J Baker?'

'That's the one. The tea rooms company. You know him?'

'Not well. I've met him though. I thought he'd been arrested for fraud?'

'Yeah.' He gave a wry smile. 'He was, but they had to let him go again as he'd done nothing wrong.'

Augusta was surprised to hear this. 'Really?'

'All the evidence pointed to a junior clerk. Granger knew nothing about it. That's what he says. Who am I to question it?'

'Do you know how he and Robson knew each other?'

'Dunno. They were both regulars here, I suppose.'

'Do you know how long they've been friends?'

'At least a year. Maybe more. I don't keep records of these things.'

It was possible Simon Granger had murdered Robert

Trigwell. Could he have murdered Douglas Robson too? Augusta decided to put the question to the landlord.

'Where was Simon Granger when Douglas Robson was murdered?'

'Just sitting over there.' He pointed at the large round table again. 'He had nothing to do with it. The police have asked me all about this and I can only tell you what I told them. Robson left this pub alone. I saw it with my own eyes. He left his friends and wished me goodnight. I was standing there.' He pointed further up the bar. 'I had a clear view of him leaving the pub and there was no one else with him. Whoever it was, they were waiting for him outside. They knew he was in here and they were lying in wait.'

'Interesting. Do you have a telephone I can use?'

Chapter 50

Mrs Hargreaves, the housekeeper, answered Miss Trigwell's telephone. 'She can't speak to you at the moment, she's having a rest.'

'It really is very urgent that I speak with her,' said Augusta. 'I'm telephoning from the King's Head pub.'

She heard the housekeeper sigh. 'Very well.' A moment later, Isabella Trigwell's weak voice came through the receiver.

'Hello?'

'Hello, Miss Trigwell. This is Mrs Peel. Did Douglas ever mention Simon Granger to you?'

'No. Who's he?'

'He worked with your brother. He was at the funeral. Tall man, square face.'

'Oh him. I remember now. Douglas knew him?'

'According to the landlord here at the King's Head, they were friends.'

'Douglas never told me that. In fact, I don't even remember them speaking at the funeral. Are you sure about this?'

'It's what the landlord tells me. Simon Granger was recently arrested for fraud at J Baker but has been released again. He was here last night when Douglas was murdered.'

'He did it?'

'No, the landlord of the pub says Mr Granger was inside the pub at the time of Douglas's murder.'

Isabella sighed. 'So he didn't do it then. Who did?'

'That's what I'm trying to find out. Are you sure Douglas never mentioned Simon's name?'

'Quite sure.'

Douglas hadn't been truthful with Isabella. Augusta decided she needed to mention another lie of his.

'Were you aware that Douglas Robson lost his job some time ago?' she asked.

'No, he didn't.'

'I'm afraid he did. I visited Albemarle and Forester and a gentleman there told me Mr Robson was dismissed last summer.'

'No! I refuse to believe it!'

'I realise it's upsetting to discover someone has been lying to you,' said Augusta. 'Perhaps he was too ashamed to admit he'd lost his job?'

'Maybe.'

'Was he relying on you for money?'

'No. He had money.'

'I wonder what his source of income was.'

'His wife, perhaps? Maybe her family had money.'

'Or his friends? This is just a theory, Isabella. But if Simon Granger was stealing money from J Baker, then perhaps he was passing some of it to Douglas.'

'Why would he do that?'

'I don't know yet. Maybe Douglas was doing some work for him.'

'He would never have been involved in any criminality!'

'Maybe he didn't realise something criminal was happening.'

'You're suggesting Douglas was involved in fraud?'

'He may have been, but perhaps he didn't realise what he was doing.' Augusta felt the need to say this to keep Isabella calm. 'But your brother noticed the fraud shortly before his death. This is the important part, Isabella. Granger knew both Robert and Douglas. I'm wondering if he could have had something to do with their deaths.'

'But you've already told me Simon Granger was in the pub when Douglas was murdered.'

'Perhaps he hired someone to do it for him?'

There was a pause on the telephone line. 'Perhaps,' said Isabella eventually. 'You think Simon Granger could be behind both murders?'

'It's possible. Perhaps Robert mentioned him before he died? Please have a think and let me know if you can remember Robert or Douglas talking about him.'

'I'll do my best. Thank you, Mrs Peel.'

Chapter 51

AUGUSTA SENT a telegram from the post office opposite Paddington railway station, then travelled by tube train to West Brompton.

Had Simon Granger murdered Robert Trigwell and Douglas Robson to cover up his fraud? Augusta had little doubt now that Douglas had been involved with the criminal scheme. Where else could he have obtained his money from? Perhaps the fraud at J Baker had been part of a bigger plot? One which Douglas had plans to use the Trigwell family money for?

Simon Granger was the one who knew the answers and Augusta felt angry he had been released by the police. Philip had warned her he was an unpleasant man and now he had persuaded the police a junior clerk had been responsible for the fraud. If he had not been released from custody, then perhaps Douglas Robson would still be alive.

These thoughts swirled in Augusta's mind as she walked through the gates of Brompton Cemetery. The long path stretched ahead of her, glistening in the rain.

The wind buffeted her umbrella as she passed the rows of tombs and walked towards the spot where Robert Trigwell had been laid to rest.

There was no headstone yet, just a patch of flattened bare earth. A book had been left on the grave. It was sodden from the rain. Augusta bent down to examine the title. *Collected Works of Aphra Behn.*

'It's my copy,' said a voice behind her.

Augusta stood up and smiled at Alfred Smith. He wore a long dark overcoat. 'You came,' she said.

'The telegram said it was urgent.' He glanced about. 'Where's Detective Inspector Fisher?'

'He's not working on the case anymore.'

'So I didn't have to come here? I thought the police had summoned me.'

'No. It was just me.'

Alfred Smith frowned. 'So what do you want?'

'I want to know the truth.'

'You know most of it,' said Alfred.

'Do I?'

'Yes. You discovered our secret. I try to visit this place most days.'

'Does Miss Golding know?'

'No. And it doesn't matter anymore. As her father said, I'm not husband material. I'm just sorry I upset her. I'll find the courage to write to her one day soon. But it won't change anything that's happened. It won't change who I am.'

Augusta didn't speak in the silence which followed. Instead, she waited for him to tell her more.

'I wish now I'd replied to his letter,' he said. 'He sent it to my parents' former address and it was forwarded to me at the medical school. That was about two months ago. His mother had died and he was distraught. I suppose that was why he wanted to contact an old friend. I was too scared to reply because I didn't want anyone else to see my letter. You hear of people being found out that way. I destroyed the one he sent me and I feel guilty I ignored him.'

'You had a reason to. You were scared.'

'Yes, I was. But I was pleased to hear from him, too. I hope he knew that I cared for him before he died. I wasn't sure if he could hear me.'

'Hear you? When?'

'I visited him on the ward. Despite what I told you, I knew he was being treated at St Thomas's after the attack. It was in the newspaper reports. So I went to see him. I knew it was risky, but I chose my time carefully and the nurses were distracted by the ward rounds at the time.'

'Did the nurses know your name? Because Robert mentioned it to them.'

'No, they didn't know who I was. I'm just a medical student in a large hospital. My name is common and not particularly memorable.'

'What happened when you visited Robert?'

'He was asleep. He was also gravely injured, and I knew then that he wouldn't…'

He tailed off and Augusta stared down at the book on the grave, waiting for him to continue.

'I'm sorry,' he said. 'This is the only time I've ever expressed my grief to someone else. You won't say anything to anyone, will you?'

'Of course not.' Augusta's throat felt tight with emotion. 'I have no right to.'

'I told him I was there and hopefully he heard me. I was able to say goodbye and I'm grateful for that. I wasn't the one who harmed him. I had no reason to. Is that why you asked me here?'

'Yes.' She met his gaze. 'And I believe you.'

'Thank you.' He wiped his eyes. 'Who did this to him?'

'I've got an idea. I just need to make some more enquiries first.'

Chapter 52

Augusta returned to the King's Head pub and ignored a whistle from a man sitting by the door. This wasn't the sort of establishment she liked to spend time in, but it was probably the easiest way to speak to Simon Granger.

'Back again?' said the landlord. 'Perhaps you'd like a drink this time?'

She asked for a brandy and took it over to the round table which she had been told Simon Granger liked to sit at. The pub was quiet. It was early evening, and she felt pleased to have got there before Granger.

There were no other women in the pub and Augusta did her best to ignore the stares from the handful of men in the place. She took a gulp of brandy to calm her nerves and felt it burn in her throat.

A wiry man in a shabby suit sauntered in and ordered a drink. Then he leant against the bar and narrowed his eyes at Augusta. 'Who are you?'

'Mrs Peel.'

'That leaves me none the wiser. What are you doing here?'

'Having a drink. Is that not allowed?'

He smiled. 'It's allowed, it's just that… well, normally we sit where you are.'

'We?'

'Me and my friends. It's our spot.'

She glanced around at the empty tables as if to suggest he was being petty.

'It sounds silly, I know,' he added. 'But it's our usual place.'

'I'm waiting for someone.'

'Who?'

'Simon Granger.'

'Simon? How do you know that's his table?'

'I just do. Have you arranged to meet him here?'

'No, not arranged nothing. But he'll be along in a minute. He always is. What do you want with him?' Then a smile crept across his face. 'You're not his new girlfriend, are you?'

'Do I look like his new girlfriend?'

'No. You're not his type.'

'That's a shame.'

He laughed and held out a cigarette packet. She declined, and he took one for himself.

'You're in luck, Mrs Peel,' he said with the cigarette between his lips. 'Here he is now.'

She turned to see the broad, square-faced man approach. He wore a dark suit and his lip raised in a sneer. 'What are you doing here?' he asked.

'That's no way to speak to your new girlfriend,' said the wiry man with a chuckle.

'Shut up, Barnes.'

'I want to speak to you about Douglas Robson,' said Augusta.

Granger shook his head. 'No, not you as well. I've had

enough of your friends, the police. Now hop it.'

'I'm sorry.'

'I said hop it, love. I'm not talking about Robson anymore.'

'What did you call me?'

'Love.'

'You didn't speak to me like that at Robert Trigwell's funeral. Why the change in tone? Is it because you're showing off in front of your friend?'

The wiry man sniggered.

'Alright, Barnes. You can hop it as well.'

Barnes moved away, and Augusta remained where she was.

Simon Granger sat opposite her and the landlord placed a pint of beer in front of him. 'What do I have to say to get rid of you?'

'Tell me who murdered Robert Trigwell and Douglas Robson.'

'I've no idea!'

'But you knew them both.'

'So everyone keeps reminding me!'

'You do realise you're going to be hassled about this until you provide evidence you weren't involved?'

'I've got alibis.'

'That might not be enough. You could have asked someone else to carry out the murders on your behalf. It's apparent to everyone now that you've been involved in criminality.'

'No it's not.' He raised his finger. 'It was a junior clerk. There's no evidence I've done anything wrong.'

'Maybe because you hire people to do things for you? If you continue to lie, then no one is going to believe a word you say. Even when you tell the truth.'

Simon Granger laughed. 'Oh really?'

'Clever criminals know that sometimes it pays to tell the truth.'

'If you're trying to get me to talk, Mrs Peel, it's not going to work.'

'What was the nature of your relationship with Douglas Robson?'

'We were friends. And I'm very upset about his death.'

'Did Mr Robson know you were stealing from your employer?'

'No. Because I wasn't. I've been unfairly dragged into all that.'

'How did he earn his money?'

'He had a few businesses.'

'Such as what?'

'I don't know the full details.'

'Were any of his businesses involved with the fraud at J Baker?'

'I wouldn't know.'

'It's interesting that you knew both murder victims.'

'Why's that interesting?'

'They must have known information which you wished to keep secret.'

He laughed. Then he lit a cigarette and blew the smoke into her face.

Augusta chose not to react.

'You're on the wrong track, Mrs Peel,' he said. 'And this pub isn't safe. Douglas Robson discovered that last night.'

Augusta kept her expression impassive. But she was mindful of Philip's warning about Simon Granger. He had told her to stay out of his way, and she had ignored his advice.

Was she being foolish now?

Over Granger's shoulder, she could see Barnes. Another man had joined him.

The risk she was taking wasn't sensible. She drained her brandy and got to her feet.

'Thank you for your time, Mr Granger.'

As soon as she was out of the pub, Augusta ran as fast as she could to Paddington railway station.

Chapter 53

'ARE YOU ALRIGHT, MRS PEEL?' asked Fred the following morning.

'Yes, I'm fine.' She leant on the counter. 'Actually, I didn't sleep very well.'

'I can look after things here if you'd like a rest.'

'That's kind of you, Fred, thank you. But it's quite alright. I have a lot to do.'

'Such as what?'

'I need to visit an ironmonger's shop which I noticed yesterday.'

'Oh.'

'And after that, as much as I'm reluctant to do it, I need to speak to Detective Sergeant Joyce.'

That afternoon, Augusta sat with Detective Sergeant Joyce in Isabella Trigwell's flat.

'You'd better have some answers,' said Miss Trigwell. 'It's been nearly three weeks since Robert was murdered and you haven't caught his killer. And if you'd caught him sooner, then he wouldn't have done the same to Douglas! You do realise you have blood on your hands?'

'I'm sorry, Miss Trigwell,' said Detective Sergeant Joyce. 'I've only just taken this case on and I can't be held responsible for my predecessor's mistakes.'

Augusta gritted her teeth and said nothing.

'You asked me about Simon Granger yesterday, Mrs Peel,' said Miss Trigwell.

'Did you?' Detective Sergeant Joyce turned to Augusta. 'You've been doing work on this case without telling me?'

'I just had some ideas,' said Augusta. 'It's why I asked you to come here this afternoon.'

Mrs Hargreaves brought in a tray with tea and cake. 'Here we are,' she said. 'This will make everyone feel better.'

'After you mentioned Simon Granger, I realised I remembered him after all,' said Miss Trigwell. 'He was definitely up to some funny business at J Baker. Robert told me about it. And Douglas told me he approached him about some money-making scheme, but he wanted nothing to do with it. Both Robert and Douglas were a threat to Simon. He must have done it.'

'Excellent!' said Detective Sergeant Joyce. 'We have a suspect!'

Augusta ignored him and accepted a cup of tea from the housekeeper. 'I don't think we can ignore the fact that Miss Trigwell has inherited an estate of around twenty-five thousand pounds.'

'What?' exclaimed Isabella, sitting forward. 'It's nowhere near that much!'

'Your solicitor says it is. And I think you know it is, too. You must have been extremely annoyed when your mother died and left the estate to your younger brother.'

'No.'

'You weren't envious that the fortune passed to your brother instead of you? Even though you're older than him? Had you been born male, then everything would have become yours. But instead, the estate, including the home you lived in, went to Robert. Not only did he become very wealthy after your mother's death, but he also owned your home. He could have asked you to leave and there would have been nothing you could have done about it.'

'He wouldn't have done that.'

'Presumably you realised that if your brother died, then the family estate would pass to you. His next closest relative.'

'I didn't think about it. I was too busy grieving for Mother. And when Robert died, I was grieving for him too. Only a cold-hearted person can think about money during such a dreadful time.'

'Douglas Robson had designs on you, didn't he?'

'What do you mean?'

'He was out of work and short of money. He took a keen interest in your family's money after the death of your brother. Your solicitor, Mr Barrington, was so concerned about it, he told Detective Inspector Fisher about it. Were you in love with Douglas Robson?'

'What a question!' Isabella lit a cigarette. 'Yes I suppose I was to begin with. And I was also fond of him as a friend. He supported me through a difficult time. I miss him enormously.'

'Did his interest in your money worry you?'

'In what way?'

'Were you concerned that he wanted to get his hands on your money?'

'No. I knew how to handle him.'

'He wanted you to sell the flat, didn't he?'

'Yes, he did. But I told him I wasn't going to.'

'Eventually, Douglas Robson became a threat, didn't he?'

Miss Trigwell laughed. 'A threat? Douglas?'

'He wasn't going to leave you alone to enjoy your money, was he? He wanted it. And he was so sure he was going to get it, that he was planning to divorce his wife and marry you. He planned to propose marriage to you. Did he wish to marry you for love? Or money?'

'I thought it was love but then I realised the truth.'

'So Mr Robson became a problem for you?'

'Just a moment!' said Detective Sergeant Joyce. 'Why are you confronting Miss Trigwell like this?'

'Because I think she's a murderer.'

'What?'

'And so is Mrs Hargreaves.'

The young detective's jaw hung open. 'If you're going to say such things, Mrs Peel, we need evidence!'

Chapter 54

'Out of all the suspects, Miss Trigwell had the strongest reason to want Robert Trigwell and Douglas Robson dead,' said Augusta.

'But just a moment,' said Detective Sergeant Joyce. 'Miss Trigwell has an alibi for the times of both murders.'

'I'm the alibi!' said Mrs Hargreaves. 'I will swear on the bible that Miss Trigwell was here in this flat when Robert and Douglas were murdered.'

'There you are, Mrs Peel,' said Detective Sergeant Joyce. 'Surely you can't doubt the word of a loyal housekeeper?'

'That's the trouble,' said Augusta. 'Mrs Hargreaves is very loyal.'

'That's a problem? What are you talking about Mrs Peel?'

'On each of my visits to this place, I've passed a little row of shops. It was only yesterday that I realised one of them is an ironmonger's store. On my way here today, I spoke to the proprietor there. I asked him if Annie Hargreaves had visited his store recently and he told me she was a regular customer. As a woman who cooked, cleaned and maintained the Trigwell home, this wasn't a surprise to me. However, the shop owner was a little surprised by something which happened recently.'

'What?' asked Detective Sergeant Joyce.

'Mrs Hargreaves bought a new kitchen knife.'

'What's so unusual about that?'

'Two weeks later, she bought another knife. Exactly the same as the first. The ironmonger was a little surprised because she'd recently bought one and the knives are good quality and should last a few years. He asked Mrs Hargreaves if there'd been anything wrong with the first one and she told him that there wasn't and that it was excellent. She told him she'd found the quality of the knife so good that she'd decided to buy a second. I asked him to show me the knife she'd purchased on both occasions. He did so, and I saw it was exactly the same type of knife which had been used to murder Robert Trigwell. A kitchen knife manufactured by Jackson's of Sheffield. Detective Inspector Fisher showed me that knife.'

'It's just a normal kitchen knife which lots of people must own!' said Miss Trigwell.

'So it's just a coincidence that Mrs Hargreaves bought two identical knives before each of the two murders?'

'Yes.'

'I'm afraid you've got this all wrong, Mrs Peel,' said Detective Sergeant Joyce. 'I have kept an open mind about both murder cases and, like you, I considered Miss Trigwell to be a suspect. But not only has Mrs Hargreaves provided her with an alibi, but also the caretaker of this building. On the evening of Douglas Robson's death, the caretaker called on each resident to tell them about maintenance works which are to be carried out in the communal areas next month. The caretaker told me he

spoke personally with Miss Trigwell. Both of them inde-
pendently verified the time as being nine o'clock in the
evening. The time of Robson's murder. She was here.'

'Thank you, Detective Sergeant Joyce, that's reassuring
to hear,' said Augusta.

'*Reassuring*? You do realise this means your entire theory
is wrong?'

'No, it doesn't. It supports it. There was presumably no
need for the caretaker to speak to Miss Trigwell, and yet he
spoke to her personally.'

'So what's your point?'

'It would have been just as well for the caretaker to
speak to Mrs Hargreaves. And it's telling that he didn't,
especially as Mrs Hargreaves usually answers the door. The
fact she didn't answer the door when he visited suggests she
wasn't here.'

'Presumably she was out on an errand of some sort.'

'Yes. Carrying out an errand for Miss Trigwell.'
Augusta turned to the housekeeper. 'Am I right?'

Mrs Hargreaves lower lip wobbled. 'I have no idea
what you're talking about, Mrs Peel.'

'You went out that evening on an errand, didn't you?
Just as Miss Trigwell asked you to. You went to the King's
Head pub and lay in wait for Douglas Robson.'

'No!' shrieked Miss Trigwell. 'I won't hear of it!'

Mrs Hargreaves covered her face.

'Mrs Peel,' said Detective Sergeant Joyce. 'This is a
ridiculous accusation. A housekeeper guilty of murder?
Are you suggesting she also murdered Robert Trigwell?'

'Yes. And I think she may also have poisoned Margaret
Trigwell.'

'You have no evidence for that!' said Miss Trigwell.

'No. But I remain convinced that you wanted the
family fortune for yourself. Douglas Robson told us your

relationship with your mother was difficult. I suspect you grew fed up with your existence here in this flat with her and wished to leave and start a new life somewhere else. France perhaps. You're fond of reading your book about the French Riviera.'

'Ridiculous!' said Miss Trigwell. 'I have no plans to move there!'

'This is little more than a deluded theory, Mrs Peel,' said Detective Sergeant Joyce. 'I think you need to leave Miss Trigwell in peace. Your accusations are upsetting.'

Mrs Hargreaves removed her hands from her face and stepped shakily into the centre of the room. 'I admit it all,' she said, her voice trembling. 'I don't want to pretend anymore. I'm tired of it. But please leave Isabella alone. She knew nothing of my plans.'

Augusta frowned. 'So what was your motive? The money would never have come to you.'

'I wanted the best for Isabella. She was so left out. She'd never married. With her family's money, she could do whatever she chose.'

'So you're saying you murdered Margaret Trigwell, Robert Trigwell and Douglas Robson without her knowledge?'

'Yes. So arrest me for it and leave Isabella alone.'

Miss Trigwell sat frozen still. Her eyes fixed on her housekeeper with a look of horror.

Chapter 55

'Well done Augusta,' said Philip on the telephone that evening. 'From what I hear, Annie Hargreaves won't stop talking. She's clearly relieved to confess. Some people who do terrible things have a great deal of trouble holding it all in. And I can't say I'm surprised.'

'Her loyalty surprises me,' said Augusta. 'She did all that for Isabella Trigwell? I'm not sure I understand what her motive was.'

'Hopefully she'll explain it all in due course.'

'Frustratingly, I didn't get it exactly right.'

'You accused the housekeeper and she confessed!'

'But I was also convinced Isabella Trigwell had something to do with it too.'

'Well you can't get everything completely right all the time, Augusta. Now I should leave you to get some rest now. You've had a very busy day.'

'How are the files you're reorganising?'

'Very dull indeed.'

'Perhaps you'll get an interesting case to work on soon, Philip.'

'I hope so, Augusta. If I prove myself to be completely hopeless at file reorganisation, then hopefully they'll put me on another investigation very soon.'

'Hopefully.' Augusta replaced the receiver, wondering when she would next see him.

Lady Hereford visited the bookshop the following morning. Her nurse pushed her bath chair up to the counter and the old lady waved a copy of the morning newspaper in her hand.

'A lowly housekeeper murdering her way through the family!' she said. 'Who'd have thought it?'

'It's an unusual case,' said Augusta.

'You did well to solve it,' said Fred.

'Yes, you did,' agreed Lady Hereford. 'You and dashing Detective Inspector Fisher.'

'I sort of solved it,' said Augusta. 'But I wasn't completely right and Philip was taken off the case.' She wondered if this was the reason she didn't feel as elated as she usually did when she had solved an investigation.

She felt like there was something missing.

'He was taken off the case?' asked Lady Hereford. 'Why?'

'So the commissioner's son could take the credit.'

'Is that so? Who's the commissioner?'

'Sir Graham Joyce.'

'I know who you mean now, I sat next to him at a dinner last year. It was a dinner to raise money for the Home for Motherless Children. Would you like me to have a word with him?'

'No, it's quite alright, Lady Hereford. I don't think Philip would appreciate us interfering.'

'I'm not suggesting interfering! Just a word. I think it's

wrong he was moved off the case to make space for Sir Graham's son. Disgraceful!'

'Would you like the bag of birdseed to feed Sparky?'

'Oh yes, please. He's been waiting there patiently, hasn't he? No sign of any rudeness at all. You've worked wonders with him, Augusta.'

The telephone rang and Augusta answered it.

'Mrs Peel? This is Isabella Trigwell,' said the voice at the other end. 'Could you please pay me a visit?'

Chapter 56

'YOU NEVER KNEW MY MOTHER, Mrs Peel.' Isabella Trigwell sat in her leather armchair dressed in black. She had recovered enough to paint her lips bright scarlet again.

'No, I didn't.'

'She wanted me to be a boy. So when Robert arrived, she doted on him. He couldn't do anything wrong in her eyes. But who was left looking after her when Father died? Me, of course. If I'd married, then perhaps it would have been different and Robert would have had to have looked after her. But I didn't marry because the men went away to war and only a few came back again. I never met the right man.'

'There's still time.'

'I don't want to marry. I've decided that now. After Father's death, Mother wallowed in self-pity. There was no room for my grief too, she wasn't interested in it. As usual, life revolved around her. Annie and I had to pander to her every need. She got worse as time went by. I was tired of it. We were both tired of it! It was as though we were sitting about in that flat with her just waiting for her to die. She was miserable, and we were miserable. It wasn't really murder, you know, she didn't have long, anyway. We merely hastened her end.'

'Who do you mean by *we?*'

'Annie and I, of course. Annie had been loyal to her for twenty years and yet you should have heard the way Mother spoke to her! As though she were no better than a piece of dirt on the sole of her shoe. I've always been fond of Annie and I didn't like seeing her being treated like that. The situation made us grow closer. Annie became closer to me than my own family. An older sister I never had.

'And as for Robert, he didn't have to put up with any of Mother's behaviour. You should have seen how much she changed when he visited! She would smile and laugh and hang on his every word. When I told him how awful she was being, he didn't believe me! I don't understand how a mother can treat her two children so differently. I still feel angry about it now, even though they're both dead and gone.'

'Are you admitting to hastening the end of your mother's life?'

'Yes. Because I don't think it's fair that Annie must take all the blame. It was brave of her to admit to her actions yesterday and I realise now that I was a coward. She was willing to accept responsibility for everything! It was selfless of her. But I don't want to be a coward. I know I'll feel better by admitting to my part too. Even if it does mean I shall end my life on the gallows. I know I will die a truthful woman and God will be my judge.'

'So, how did you murder your mother?'

'We decided on poison. I'm happy to tell the police that Annie and I added arsenic to her food and drink until we found the right dose. There really was nothing more to it than that. She was already in a weakened state, so she succumbed after a week or so. I know there's talk about exhuming her, but I really don't want that to happen. I'm fearful it will free her troubled spirit and she'll haunt us! I know it sounds ridiculous, but I think she needs to remain in the ground.'

'And what about Robert's murder?'

'It was my idea. We were never close, and it angered me he inherited everything. So you were right about that.'

'I struggle to believe Annie could be brutal enough to attack him in that way.'

'I offered her a lot of money.' Isabella smiled. 'Annie's worked hard all her life and has little to show for it. I told her we could split the fortune once it became mine.'

'So you were offering her a sum of twelve and a half thousand pounds?'

'Something like that. I didn't know how much it would be until the solicitor confirmed it. But I knew it would be a lot. I told Annie that getting rid of Robert was our only hope if we were to be rich.'

'So Annie had a strong incentive to attack your brother.'

'Yes, she did. We were both very worried when we discovered he had been taken to hospital. We felt sure he'd recover and tell everyone who attacked him. But it seems he didn't really recover enough to talk properly. He mentioned Alfred Smith, and that was it. We got away with it.'

'How did Annie know he would be in the cloisters of Westminster Abbey?'

'It was a favourite place of his. He liked to sit there in quiet contemplation, close to the resting place of Aphra Behn. My brother wasn't a bad man, he just did nothing to help me. And after Mother died, he had the power to take everything away from me.'

'And Annie attacked Douglas too?'

'Yes. When he went to the King's Head, she waited for him outside. When he came out, she told him she needed a quiet word. And then she attacked him. She had no qualms about it at all. We had to stop Douglas. He was after my money, as you rightly pointed out yesterday, Mrs Peel. You're a clever woman. I like clever women. Under different circumstances, I think we could have become friends. What do you think?'

'Possibly.' Augusta had no wish to be Isabella Trigwell's friend. 'I appreciate you taking the time to explain everything to me. And thank you for speaking so honestly.'

'I think you already knew it, anyway. I realised it was foolish of me to continue keeping quiet and it seemed so unfair to make Annie take the blame for everything. Perhaps we'll be put together in neighbouring cells? I'm missing her dreadfully. Please can you inform Scotland Yard that I'm ready and waiting for them here?'

'I'll use your telephone if I may.'

'Of course.'

Augusta went to the telephone in the hallway and asked to be put through to Scotland Yard. She then told Philip that Isabella Trigwell had made a confession.

'Gosh. Really? That's marvellous, Augusta! So you were right to suspect her after all. I'll get a cab right now. It's going to take me about twenty minutes to get there. Make sure she doesn't go anywhere.'

'You must have somewhere to go,' said Isabella Trigwell when Augusta returned to the living room.

'No, I don't. I'll wait here until Detective Inspector Fisher arrives.'

Augusta didn't want to leave Isabella unattended.

Isabella's eyes looked darker. She had been conversational and compliant until now, but her mood was changing. 'I would like you to leave,' she said.

'And I want to keep an eye on you until Detective Inspector Fisher gets here.'

'Fine.' Isabella got up from her chair and left the room. Augusta got up and followed. Isabella walked through the hallway and into the kitchen. Augusta guarded the front door, assuming it was the only exit from the flat. They were on the fourth storey, so she felt sure Isabella wouldn't try to escape through a window.

Some time passed before Augusta decided to look for Isabella in the kitchen. There was no sign of her there or in the dining room. Augusta looked around some more. There were two bedrooms, and both were empty. The bathroom door was locked.

Everything was silent.

'Isabella?' called out Augusta.

There was no reply.

'Is everything alright?'

She didn't like the idea of bothering someone in the bathroom, but something didn't feel right. The hairs on the back of her neck prickled.

Chapter 57

'Isabella!'

There was still no reply.

Augusta paced around the flat. Although Isabella had every right to use the bathroom in peace, Augusta felt sure something was wrong. Had Isabella gone into the bathroom because it was the only room with a lockable door?

Augusta tried the door handle. 'Isabella! Please tell me you're alright.'

She pushed against the door, but it wouldn't budge.

Had Isabella harmed herself?

The door was thick and solid. She wasn't sure she could break it down.

She ran to the telephone to call a doctor. Although how a doctor could tend to Miss Trigwell when she was beyond a locked door, Augusta couldn't be sure.

Just as she picked up the receiver, there was a knock at the door.

'Oh, Philip!' she gasped, to his obvious surprise. 'Thank goodness you're here! I'm worried about Isabella. She's locked herself in the bathroom.'

'That's allowed, isn't it?'

'She won't respond when I call her name. I'm worried she's harmed herself.'

Panic flashed across his face, and she led him to the bathroom door.

'It's locked and it won't budge!' She tried it again.

'Miss Trigwell?' he called out. 'Detective Inspector Philip Fisher here! Can you hear us?' Silence. 'We're worried about you. Can you open the door?'

Augusta held her breath as they waited for a reply.

'How long has she been in there?' he asked.

'I don't know. Ten minutes. Maybe fifteen.'

'I call that long enough.' He tried the handle of the door and called out. 'Miss Trigwell, we're concerned about your welfare and, for that reason, I'm going to attempt to gain entry. If you can hear me and are near the door, please move back from it now!'

He turned to Augusta. 'There's no word from her is there? I'm going to have to get in there. Can you hold this for me, please?' He handed her his walking stick, then propped one hand against the door frame while he pummelled below the door handle with the side of his fist. Augusta heard a crack in the door frame, but the door refused to give way.

Philip took a step back. 'I can't believe she's not reacted to that racket. This is worrying indeed. I'm going to have to kick the door with my heel.'

'But you can't! Your leg won't be up to it.'

'Curse this leg!'

'How about I try?'

He looked down at her smart skirt. 'But your clothing restricts you, Augusta.'

'Then you're going to have to look away while I kick the door.'

'Do you think you can do it?'

'I don't know. But I have to try, don't I?'

'And you have sturdy shoes on. They should help. Right, if you think you can do it, then you'll need to aim your heel where the latch is. The door handle is in the way, so you'll have to do your best not to hit it. Some short, sharp jabs with your heel should hopefully do the trick, but you'll need to get all your weight behind it. I'll stand behind you and catch you if you lose your balance.'

'Right.' Augusta took in a breath and prepared herself. 'I'll need to hitch my skirt up above my knee.'

'I'll look away.' He moved behind her. 'I'll just look at the back of your head.'

Augusta stared at the spot on the door in front of her. If Isabella had harmed herself, then every wasted minute was bringing her closer to death.

'Ready?' she said to Philip.

'Yes. Now kick down that door!'

Augusta shifted her weight onto her left leg, hitched up her skirt and felt a little embarrassed that she was exposing the top of her stocking. Then she raised her right leg and used all the strength she could muster to propel her heel into the door. She felt it shift beneath her foot, but pain shot up into her hip as she stumbled to get her balance again.

'Well done!' shouted Philip.

She tried again. But this time, the strength seemed to have left her. Her heel made contact with the door, but with little impact.

'Never mind!' said Philip. 'Give it another go!'

Augusta took in a breath and thought of Isabella's confession. They needed her to face justice. She couldn't be allowed to slip away peacefully. Her victims hadn't been allowed to.

She hitched up her skirt and raised her right leg again. For the third time, she drove her heel into the door. There was another crack, but still it didn't open.

Her right leg felt weak now. She knew those three attempts were the best she could do.

'Almost there,' said Philip. 'Can you manage another one?'

'No,' she puffed.

'I see. I think we're going to need help from someone—'

'There isn't time to fetch help. We need to get in there now!' With a cry, Augusta launched her shoulder at the door, her entire weight behind it.

The frame splintered, the door flung open, and she fell inside.

Isabella was lying face down on the floor by the bathtub. Her face was turned to Augusta. Her eyes were closed and her lips blue.

Augusta called out her name as she scrambled over to her. She grabbed her wrist and felt for a pulse. 'Isabella!' She slapped her fingers gently on her cheek, but there was no response.

'Good grief,' said Philip. 'Is she alive?'

'I don't know yet.' She tried again to feel for a pulse.

Philip stepped over to the sink. 'A little mirror,' he said, handing it to Augusta. 'Hold it by her nose and mouth.' Augusta did so. They waited for a moment and eventually the edge of the mirror clouded.

'She's breathing!' said Augusta. 'She's alive!'

'At the moment she is,' said Philip. 'But that could change. I'll call a doctor.'

Chapter 58

PHILIP CALLED at the bookshop the following day. 'Apparently Isabella Trigwell has had a comfortable night,' he said. 'Or as comfortable as is possible after consuming bleach.'

'Bleach?' said Fred. 'That's rather drastic.'

'After confessing to three murders, she clearly decided she didn't want to stand trial for them,' said Augusta. 'But hopefully she'll recover enough to be tried alongside Annie Hargreaves.'

'I'm sure she will,' said Philip. 'And you'll be pleased to hear Simon Granger has been arrested again. Sergeant Hamilton tells me they're planning to charge him over the fraud.'

'Excellent!'

'Good old Hamilton obtained the statements from Granger's personal bank account and identified a series of deposits which matched the withdrawals from J Baker. There were also payments from his account being made to Mr D Robson. Quite substantial sums too.'

'So Granger and Robson were up to something.'

'Just as you suspected. We'll find out the details in due course. So well done for finishing off the case, Augusta. I knew you could do it.'

'It would have been easier if you hadn't been moved to file organising.'

'Yes, it would. Well, thankfully, there'll be no more of that.'

'You've been given an interesting case to work on?'

'Not exactly.' He rubbed his brow. 'I thought I should come and tell you something. Before you hear it from anyone else.'

Augusta didn't like the serious look on his face. 'What is it?'

'I met with the commissioner this morning and tendered my resignation.'

Augusta felt her mouth drop open. 'You're leaving Scotland Yard?'

'I'm afraid so.'

'But you weren't even there long. Barely three years!'

'You're right. I was offered the position at the end of the war. But I don't think I'm really cut out for it.'

'Of course you are! You've done a lot of work for them and caught a lot of criminals! The Yard has been lucky to have you.'

Philip smiled. 'You don't need to flatter me, Augusta.'

'I'm not! I'm merely stating the truth.'

'Well, your words are kind indeed. My time at the Yard has been interesting and the pressures of the job have certainly seen off my marriage.'

'That's the reason you're leaving? Because your marriage ended?'

'No. I suspect my marriage was going to end, anyway. My wife would have found another reason, I'm sure.'

Philip's resignation felt difficult to accept. If he no

longer worked at the Yard, Augusta would have no reason to see him again.

'You look sad, Augusta.'

'That's because I am! I know I've occasionally been a reluctant sleuth, but I've enjoyed our time working together.'

'So have I.'

'It won't be the same.'

'No, it won't. It will be quite different.' He smiled.

'You seem pleased about that.'

'I am.'

'Why?'

'Because of what the future holds.'

'And what does the future hold?'

'None of us can know for sure, can we?'

'But you're planning something. You have an enigmatic smile on your face, Philip. Please tell me what you're up to.'

'Well, my plans to leave the Yard aren't as hasty as they might seem.'

'You've been thinking about this for a while?'

'Yes.'

'Why didn't you say anything?'

'Because we've been busy trying to catch a murderer. And also I wanted to be sure about my plan before I mentioned anything to you.'

'So what is it?'

'I plan to establish a detective agency.'

Augusta smiled. 'Really?' Suddenly, his idea to leave the Yard seemed like a sensible one. 'You're going to set up on your own? You'll be brilliant at it, Philip!'

He laughed. 'I'm pleased you think so. Fisher's Detective Agency. It has quite a ring to it. Don't you think?'

'It does!'

'I think you'll be a brilliant private detective,' said Fred.

'So when will you start?' asked Augusta.

'As soon as possible. I have to work my notice at the Yard and then I'm free. I'll need to find an office, though.'

'Whereabouts?'

'I don't mind. Central London somewhere.'

'Bloomsbury maybe?'

'Bloomsbury's good.' Philip turned to Fred. 'I'm looking for some recently vacated offices above a second-hand bookshop run by an eccentric book repairing lady who keeps a canary for company. Do you know of any?'

Fred laughed. 'Now you come to mention it, I think I do.'

'Eccentric?' protested Augusta.

Philip grinned. 'In a nice way.'

'So you're going to take the offices above this shop?'

'I'd be foolish not to, wouldn't I?'

'Yes, you would.' She couldn't stop smiling.

'And if possible, I'd like you close at hand, Augusta. Just in case I need some help with a case or two. You never know, do you?'

The End

Historical Note

The first church was built on the site of Westminster Abbey nearly 1,000 years ago by Edward the Confessor, King of England from 1042 to 1066. The current building was built by Henry III in the 13th century and Edward the Confessor's tomb was placed in a shrine. It's still there today.

Around 30 monarchs and consorts are buried in the Abbey and over 100 poets and writers are either buried or memorialised there. Among the famous writers buried in Poet's Corner are Geoffrey Chaucer, Edmund Spenser, Ben Jonson, John Dryden, Samuel Johnson, Robert Browning, Alfred, Lord Tennyson, Rudyard Kipling, and Thomas Hardy. There are no women buried in Poet's Corner, the closest is Aphra Behn in the abbey cloisters.

I feel some attachment to the Abbey because I've climbed on its roof. I should add there was scaffolding on it at the time. It was a fascinating and wobbly experience because, like Augusta, I struggle with heights. The roof exploration was something I did as a student when learning about the Abbey's major restoration project (it ran from 1973 to 95).

In recent times, the Abbey has been the location for the funeral of Queen Elizabeth II and the coronation of King Charles III.

Aphra Behn was a 17th century poet and writer. She's said to be one of the first English women to earn her living from writing. Her plays were popular with audiences, and she became one of the leading playwrights in England. Her plays were praised for her wit and her originality and sometimes criticised for her bawdy humour. She wrote over eighteen plays along with poetry, prose fiction, and translations. Her most famous work of fiction is Oroonoko (1688), a short novel about an enslaved African prince. Oroonoko is considered to be one of the first novels in English to explore slavery. She died in 1689 at the age of 48.

St Thomas's Hospital dates back to 1173, when it was founded as a medieval infirmary named after St Thomas Becket. In the 19th century, it became a centre for medical education and research. Florence Nightingale, the pioneer of modern nursing, worked at St Thomas's and significantly improved nursing practices there. The current building opened in 1871 and occupied a prominent position on the south bank of the River Thames - opposite the Houses of Parliament.

The hospital buildings have been added to over the years, but a large part of the 1870s building still stands. The hospital remains one of the largest and busiest in central London.

St Thomas's Medical school was founded in the 1550s and is now part of the GKT School of Medical Education at King's College London.

The WWI Battle of the Somme began on 1st July 1916. On that morning, the 8th Battalion of the Royal East Surrey Regiment launched their attack from their trenches at Carnoy, northern France. Captain Wilfred Percy 'Billie' Nevill and platoon commander Lieutenant Robert Eley Soames led the charge, kicking footballs, aiming to score a 'goal' in the enemy trenches. Some reports say there were two footballs, others say there were four. Two footballs were recovered from the battlefield.

That day on the Somme was the deadliest day in history for the British Army. 120,000 men left their trenches on the morning of 1st July 1916. Tragically, 21,000 of them were killed within thirty minutes. By the end of the day, the British Army had suffered 57,470 casualties.

Captain Nevill and Lieutenant Soames lost their lives during their football charge. Both were just twenty-one years old.

After the war, the two footballs were displayed in museums. One was in the Surrey Infantry Museum in Clandon Park, Surrey. The building suffered a devastating fire in 2015 and sadly, the football was destroyed along with many other items.

The remaining football survives and is in the collection at the Princess of Wales's Royal Regiment Museum in Dover Castle.

The impressive old War Office building in Whitehall opened in 1906. Secretaries of State for War who worked in the building during its early years included Herbert Asquith, Lord Kitchener, David Lloyd George and Winston Churchill. As government departments were reorganised over the years, staff were moved to more modern offices. By the turn of the century, the building was falling into disrepair. It was sold by the Ministry of Defence in 2013 and (at the time of writing in September 2023) is about to open as a very swanky-looking Raffles hotel. A night's stay will start at £1,000.

The war records from WWI were moved to a War Office warehouse - the Army Records Centre - in south London in the 1930s. The area was heavily bombed in September 1940 during WWII. During the bombardment, the Army Records Centre caught fire and most of its records were lost. It was estimated that out of 6.5 million documents, 1.25 million survived. As a result, many people researching a British ancestor who fought in WWI will only find limited information about their family member's service.

Thank you

Thank you for reading *Death in Westminster* I really hope you enjoyed it!

Would you like to know when I release new books? Here are some ways to stay updated:

- Like my Facebook page: facebook.com/emilyorganwriter
- Follow me on Goodreads: goodreads.com/emily_organ
- Follow me on BookBub: bookbub.com/authors/emily-organ
- View my other books here: emilyorgan.com or scan the code on the next page.

Thank you

Also by Emily Organ

Penny Green Series:

Limelight
The Rookery
The Maid's Secret
The Inventor
Curse of the Poppy
The Bermondsey Poisoner
An Unwelcome Guest
Death at the Workhouse
The Gang of St Bride's
Murder in Ratcliffe
The Egyptian Mystery
The Camden Spiritualist

Churchill & Pemberley Series:

Tragedy at Piddleton Hotel
Murder in Cold Mud
Puzzle in Poppleford Wood

Also by Emily Organ

Trouble in the Churchyard
Wheels of Peril
The Poisoned Peer
Fiasco at the Jam Factory
Disaster at the Christmas Dinner
Christmas Calamity at the Vicarage (novella)

Writing as Martha Bond

Lottie Sprigg Series:

Murder in Venice
Murder in Paris
Murder in Cairo
Murder in Monaco
Murder in Vienna

Limelight

A Penny Green Mystery Book 1

~

How did an actress die twice?

Penny Green has lost her job. Once admired as Fleet Street's first lady reporter, she's been dismissed for criticising a police decision. So when Scotland Yard calls on her help in a murder case, she's reluctant to assist.

But the case perplexes her. How was a famous Victorian actress shot in Highgate Cemetery five years after she drowned in the River Thames? It makes no sense.

Penny's personal connection to the murdered actress draws her in. As does the charm of Scotland Yard inspector, James Blakely. But her return to work sparks the attentions of someone with evil intent. Who is so desperate to keep the past hidden?

Find out more here: mybook.to/penny-green-limelight

Tragedy at Piddleton Hotel

A Churchill & Pemberley Mystery Book 1

A discarded tea cake causes a fatal fall. An accident? Or was it purposefully placed? Two elderly ladies task themselves with a puzzling case.

When widowed Annabel Churchill leaves London and buys a detective agency in the village of Compton Poppleford, she's faced with a murder investigation. Teaming up with eccentric spinster, Doris Pemberley, she vows to crack it.

The death of local busybody, Mrs Furzgate, at the local hotel leaves the villagers vexed and the constabulary clueless. Churchill and Pemberley fuel themselves with cake and quiz a range of local characters. What's the connection with Mr Bodkin the baker? And why did Mrs Furzgate fall out with the Women's Compton Poppleford Bridge Club?

It's soon apparent that many people bore Mrs Furzgate a grudge. But when Inspector Mappin accuses the senior sleuths of meddling, they're in danger of never finding the killer…

Find out more here: mybook.to/tragedy-hotel

Printed in Great Britain
by Amazon